A Bed and Breakfast Affair

Joanne McGough

SILVERBEAR GRAPHICS
Stahlstown, Pennsylvania

© 2012 by Joanne McGough. All Rights Reserved. No part of this book may be reproduced in any form or by any electronic or mechanical means, including information storage and retrieval systems, without permission in writing from the author, except by a reviewer who may quote brief passages in a review, or for eBook use according to the rules and regulations of the e publication system through which the eBook was legally purchased.

To obtain permission for reprint or to contact the author email contact the author at:

joanne.mcgough@silverbeargraphics.com

Published by Silverbear Graphics
647 Jones Mills Stahlstown Road
Stahlstown, PA 15687
www.silverbeargraphics.com

First Edition: 18 March 2012 Paperback
Printed in the United States of America

McGough, Joanne

A Bed and Breakfast Affair

ISBN: 978-0-9847087-4-1
Library of Congress Control Number: 2011945631

Dedication

To everyone who encouraged me to write, and to friends in Beanery Writers and Joe's Critique Group, my everlasting gratitude.

Chapter 1

Howth, County Dublin, Ireland

Mrs. Emma Quinn was busy, though it was early in June. As a Bed and Breakfast proprietor, she did not expect to have many paying guests at the top of the month, largely because of the weather.

Early June was usually chilly and rainy. Emma cautioned her guests that a morning outing required the wearing of a warm woolen sweater and stout shoes. To venture out in the evening, one should don a coat, wear a hat and, of course, stout shoes. Having an umbrella close at hand was a necessity at all times, day and night.

Later in the month there would still be rain, but not every day and not all day long. This was the best time of year in Emma Quinn's opinion. She thought the term 'Emerald Isle' must have been coined in late June, when the greening of the land comes to its fullness. That was when the tourist season really began. But here she was on June fifth with six paying guests.

Emma's husband, Tommy, was a faithful man, but he was a man who liked his whiskey. Some mornings he couldn't get up for work because he had liked his whiskey too much the night before. And so to make ends meet, Emma opened her home to tourists.

In 1960, eight years ago, she notified the Board F'ealte of her intention. She put a sign on her lawn that said,

SEA VIEW
B&B
Mrs. E. Quinn, Prop.

Her home was modest compared to other Bed and Breakfast homes, but it was a detached house, unusual in a small Irish village. One walked on a path through the lawn and garden to Sea View's front door. Inside, a small foyer with a long hallway led to the open kitchen.

On the right side of the hall was the sliding door to the parlor. Another sliding door inside the parlor opened to the dining room. At breakfast and tea time these doors were kept open for guests. At all other times they were closed, for this was a family home, after all.

The dining room opened to the kitchen, so Emma could easily go back and forth with trays of food.

The rooms on the ground floor of Sea View were very large. The house had central heating, but Ireland's persistent dampness always caused a chill. Each room had a fireplace nook, which burned coal and was used even in June.

On the left side of the foyer were the stairs to the upper floor. The stairs changed direction at the top, reaching a central hall. The guest rooms, two smallish doubles, two small singles, and one bathroom were entered from this hall. Emma's bedroom was at the very end.

It was a functional house, not remarkable in any way. But Emma intended to have a profitable business. Therefore, she focused on providing her guests with excellent food and service. She prided herself on being observant, thus giving individualized care. She quickly ascertained whether a guest preferred coffee or tea with breakfast, how they liked their breakfast eggs cooked and if they usually chose bacon, sausage or ham. She knew if a guest was chatty in the morning or quiet until the second cup of coffee came.

Besides providing bed and breakfast, Emma enjoyed serving afternoon tea to her guests. She joined them at the dining room table, for she delighted in hearing people talk about their homes and lives. She loved pouring tea and passing the plate full of scones, all the while studying the idiosyncrasies of each person. Little did she know that her warm, observant nature would soon be of help to a prominent garda detective.

Emma knew that the village Howth gave her a great advantage in the Bed and Breakfast industry. Howth, beautifully situated by the Irish Sea with long piers that project into the sea like giant fingers, was indeed picturesque. Also, it was only nine miles north of Dublin, perfect for tourists who wanted to shop and sightsee in the cosmopolitan city, but spend their nights in a quieter local.

Howth could be the village on a picture post card. On the High Street were many shops owned and operated by local people: the green grocer's shop, the fish monger, the butcher shops (one for chicken, one for lamb and pork). Their open windows, no flies, minimal refrigeration and their wooden floors always amazed Americans. No supermarket here.

Other shops sold locally-made cottage industry goods. Intricately knitted Aran Isle sweaters, woven blankets, silver jewelry and Arklow pottery all drew many tourists and their money.

Added to all this, there were two well-known restaurants in Howth, both near Emma's home. The Royal Howth Hotel, just up the road from Sea View, offered an haute cuisine experience, and many famous people stayed here.

Across the cobblestone street and down toward the pier a bit was the Abbey Tavern, known for its beef dishes and its singing barn. Guests finished their dinners, and then took their drinks out to the barn to hear the Abbey Tavern singers perform songs of war and love.

Also, Emma knew there was a sort of grapevine communication among Bed and Breakfast tourists. For example, Mr. and Mrs. John Doe might meet Mr. and Mrs. Tom Smith at a B&B in Galway. Upon learning that the Smiths were going to spend a few days in Dublin, the Does might say, "Do drive to Howth and stay with Mrs. Quinn at Sea View. She's a wonderful hostess." Thus the good reputation of Sea View was made.

Of course, this year, as in the eight previous years, Major Arthur Fitzgerald was there. Late in May, someone from the Board F'ealte rang up Mrs. Quinn and asked if she could accommodate a single gentleman from Waterford for the first two weeks of June. She always agreed, and the pattern was always the same. On June first he arrived, and on June fifteenth he left, keeping to himself every day, polite but private.

Some years the major was Mrs. Quinn's only guest for these two weeks. And some years there were one or two other guests. But never before had Sea View been full up this early in the month. Her five other guests were an interesting lot.

On June second, the two women from Scotland arrived. The Board had phoned the day before about their reservation. They arrived in a rented Volkswagen late in the afternoon, Miss Jean Blair and Mrs. Mary MacGregor.

Jean Blair was average in height, weight, appearance, personality. To Emma, she seemed meek and willing to take a back seat to her companion.

Mary MacGregor was a tall redhead, lovely really. She was widowed three years earlier. She and Jean worked together at the Royal Bank of Scotland in Stranraer. Both women had Scotland passports.

The next day, June third, an American couple arrived. They wrote for reservations three months before. They were John and Kitty Murphy. He was a policeman in Boston, Massachusetts, she a homemaker. Emma had reserved her nicest double room for them, for she found Americans to be fussier about small details than Europeans generally were.

Later that same day a young Welshman knocked at her door and asked if she had a single room. His name was Gwillam Morgan, and he was a schoolmaster from Rhyll, a small town in northern Wales. Emma offered him her small, single room—smaller than the room Major Fitzgerald always occupied. Morgan said the room was acceptable, and he carried his luggage in.

Thus, Emma Quinn had a full house. She had six pleasant, polite and seemingly innocuous guests. She had no need to be concerned about anyone.

chapter 2

On Tuesday, June fifth, Emma got an early start to her day. She was up at six thirty a.m. to get her husband up, fed and off to work. She had just enough time to make a second cup of tea for herself and sip from it as she laid the table for her guests' eight a.m. breakfast. She set only five places at the table, however, knowing Major Fitzgerald preferred to breakfast alone in his room.

This year, as in the eight previous years, Emma prepared the major's breakfast and carried the tray up to his room at eight thirty a.m. She appreciated his patronage, so she gave this extra bit of service without complaining.

Gwillam Morgan came downstairs to breakfast before the others. Morgan did not look like the typical Welshman. He was tall and sandy-haired, with a sprinkling of freckles on his face. But his melodic speaking voice left no doubt as to his nationality. Emma thought that he might be about forty years old.

Emma welcomed Gwillam to take any seat he wanted at the table, but he said he would wait a while if she didn't mind. They chatted while she laid the table settings. She thought him to be quite amiable.

She guessed why he wasn't sitting yet. Yesterday morning and again yesterday at tea, Morgan managed to claim a seat next to Mary MacGregor. Emma couldn't blame him. The Scots widow was young, probably about thirty-five years old, in Emma's estimation. And she was very lovely. She had shoulder length, wavy red hair, and the alabaster white skin that one associated more with Irish genes than Scottish.

Mary and Jean were next to come down to breakfast. Jean greeted Emma and Gwillam with a friendly 'Good morning,' then seated herself at the table.

Poor plain girl, Emma thought. *Not the sort a man would take much notice of. Still, she's friendlier than her gorgeous friend.*

Mary took her seat next to Jean, and Gwillam sat next to Mary.

Emma chuckled to herself. The looks on Mary and Gwillam's faces, their smiles for each other, left no doubt about the attraction they both felt.

Emma envied them. She hadn't felt loved for a long time. Tommy was so deep into his alcoholism that he never showed her any love, or even affection. She could not even recall the last time they had loved as man and wife, it was that long ago. She wondered if she would ever have that love from a man again. It certainly wasn't going to come from Tommy.

John Murphy came to the dining room in a burst of energy and noise, greeting the others effusively. He was a well-meaning man, but much too familiar with others, a typical American, in Emma's opinion. His greeting to Emma this morning was the same as yesterday, which was that Kitty would be down soon.

Emma did not like Kitty Murphy. She thought the woman bitter and quarrelsome. Emma was certain that Kitty was suspicious of her husband and kept a close watch on that big, ginger-haired man.

It was nearly twenty after eight yesterday morning when Kitty made her way to breakfast. She looked silly to Emma, wearing blue eye shadow from her eye lashes to her eyebrows. She also wore lipstick of a defiant red shade which stained the cloth napkins and stayed on her coffee cup. Today, Emma expected a repeat performance. Indeed, Kitty presented herself at eight-twenty a.m.

Emma served a bountiful, well-cooked breakfast to her guests. She poured each person's first cup of coffee or tea and didn't have to ask which they preferred. She left pots of each brew on the table so her guests could help themselves to more. Then she went back to the kitchen to begin the major's meal.

From her kitchen, she could easily watch the people at the table. She happened to see John Murphy staring at Mary. As if in silent communication, Mary looked up from her meal and met his gaze. The expression on her face didn't reveal any emotion, but Emma observed her rather abrupt attempt to start a conversation with Gwillam Morgan. Emma wondered if Kitty Murphy had seen her husband staring at Mary. She hoped not, for John's sake.

Emma found herself thinking about Mary MacGregor and Jean Blair. They were young, still in their thirties. She imagined their lives to be carefree, with plenty of time for fun. Emma recently celebrated her fortieth birthday.

I'm not much older than they are, she thought. She felt old. What with Tommy's drinking and the hard work of running her business, she felt stressed and tired.

But she had not time for daydreaming. She still had to get the major's breakfast up to him, clear the table, wash the dishes, and then set about cleaning the guests' rooms and bathroom. She thought her friend, Frances Houlihan, should be arriving soon. At least Emma would have some help with the morning work.

chapter 3

While her guests lingered over second cups of coffee and tea, Emma prepared a breakfast tray for Major Arthur Fitzgerald and took it upstairs to his room. As usual, she knocked softly on his door and then set the tray of food on the table outside his room. That task accomplished, she went downstairs and busied herself in the kitchen.

Where is that Francie? she thought. Emma's friend and neighbor, Frances Houlihan, was expected at eight a.m. daily when Emma was "full up." Even though Francie was past fifty, she was a great worker. She helped serve the breakfast, wash up dishes and clean the guests' rooms.

She's probably listening to some gossip somewhere! Emma thought.

Emma knew Francie well. Emma was glad for her friend's help and paid her a little something to show her appreciation. But Francie's habit of absorbing gossip annoyed Emma. On quiet days, when the two friends could sit and relax, Emma would find herself amused at her friend's version of recent tales she'd heard. And as long as Francie stayed away from the subject of Emma's disappointing marriage to a drinker, Emma was content to let her rattle on. But on busy days! Really!

Wouldn't you think the woman would have enough sense to come directly to work? Ah, she's probably chit-chatting somewhere!

When the kitchen things were done and the guests had all gone out sightseeing and shopping, Emma decided that she might was well set about tidying up their rooms and started on her work. As she walked by the major's room, she noticed that his breakfast try sat untouched on the table outside his door.

Oh my, the major didn't hear my knock, she decided, and she rapped on his door again, a good bit louder this time.

First she went to Mr. Morgan's room, the easiest because it was a single. Fairly neat, Mr. Morgan was. The window in his room was open, for the Welshman found the Irish weather to be not much different from that at home. Emma straightened up the bed, dusted the furniture and Hoovered the carpet. She scoured the sink, polished the mirror and replaced the used towels with clean, fresh ones.

Next, the guests' bathroom. As in most B&Bs, all the guests at Sea View shared a common bathroom. No one could have complained about the cleanliness of this room, for Emma Quinn scrubbed it daily. Most people adjusted easily to sharing bathroom facilities—most people, but not Kitty Murphy. The day the Murphys arrived at Sea View they argued bitterly about staying there, even though they had written for reservations three months in advance. Kitty whined and pleaded, "I can't stay in a place where I have to share a toilet and tub with strangers! I refuse! Please, please can't we move to a hotel?"

John Murphy stood his ground.

"Damn it, Kitty, we're staying here! The Burkes said this is the best B&B they found and we're staying! "

When the bathroom was clean enough to satisfy her, Emma Quinn went to tidy up the Murphy's room. But when she walked into that room and saw the general disarray, she decided to let it go until later.

Maybe Francie will finally show up and give me a hand with that mess, she hoped.

So Mrs. Quinn went instead to the room shared by the two Scots women. As she turned in the direction of their room, she noticed the breakfast tray still outside the major's door.

By now, ten thirty a.m., the food was cold and the meal was ruined. Emma was quite puzzled, to say the least. For eight years now, every June, from the first day of the month to the fifteenth day of the month, at eight-thirty a.m. she had prepared a breakfast tray for Major Arthur Fitzgerald, set it outside his door, knocked on the door and left. Two hours later, each day without exception, the major would leave his room for the second time. He always bid a "Good Day" to her and to Francie and went out for the day. Had she heard him leave at seven o'clock that morning? She couldn't be sure. Did he return at eight o'clock? She didn't notice. Major Fitzgerald could have returned to Sea View at the usual time or later, while her other guests were eating breakfast and she was busy attending to them. No one was paying any particular attention.

Emma thought about the situation and decided that if she didn't see the major leave soon, she would enter his room.

Maybe he's a bit under the weather, she guessed.

Then, as she checked the time again, another thought reoccurred. *Where is that Francie Houlihan?*

Mrs. Quinn left the door to Major Fitzgerald's room and went across the hall to the room shared by Mary MacGregor and Jean Blair. Everything neat there. Both beds had already been made by the ladies themselves. Their luggage was neatly stacked in a corner. Each lady had good leather luggage in a natural leather color, not hot pink like a certain American lady's. Their toiletry articles were neatly arranged on the dresser top, Mrs. MacGregor's subtle but expensive French cologne on the left, Miss Blair's nondescript American toilet water on the right. After a quick Hoovering, a light dusting and a good airing, Emma found herself all too soon finished in this room. She had nothing left to do but clean the Murphy's mess next door.

By now, eleven a.m., Emma was very angry with Francie Houlihan.

If she does show up I'll fire her, thought Emma, indignantly.

The Murphy's room was really too much. Bed unmade! Blue eye shadow on the pillow case! Emma had to replace that pillow case daily. Toothpaste and shaving cream left drying in the sink! A wet cake of soap lying on the floor! And the dresser top—Kitty Murphy's face powder spilled all over it!

Emma attacked this messy room and in about half an hour's time had it looking respectable.

Only till tomorrow morning, she thought, *when I'll have to do it all over again.*

Emma had done all the morning's cleaning by herself. By the time she was finished, she was fairly tired, but she was also worried about two puzzling situations that were occurring that morning. First, what had become of Francie Houlihan? And what should she do about Major Fitzgerald and his untouched breakfast?

Emma walked to the door of the major's room and stood there for a minute, some conflicting thoughts weighing on her mind.

What if he's sick? She wondered. *I should go in and see. But what if he would rather not be bothered? Surely, this is a man who likes his privacy.*

Finally, her concern for the major's welfare won out over her fear of intruding on him. She knocked on his door. She waited. She knocked again, louder. She waited. She took her pass key from her apron pocket, pushed the key into the lock and shouted, "I'm coming in!" But the sound of her words was completely drowned out by the explosive arrival of Francie Houlihan!

chapter 4

Francie Houlihan came bursting into Sea View screeching like a banshee and looking like a wild thing. Her small, wiry body never did fill out her clothes, and now her cotton dress was twisted like a corkscrew all about her bony frame. Her gray hair was loose and frenzied. Hairpins were falling over her face.

"Emma, Emma! Where are ya woman? Oh, Emma! Ya won't believe wha' 'appened," she screamed.

"Frances Houlihan, you've a nerve showing up at noon when I expected you here three hours ago! I've a good mind to fire you!" Emma scolded, hurrying down the stairs.

"Ah, hush woman and listen to me!" Francie's voice trailed behind her, for she was on her way to the kitchen.

"Francie, you stand still when I'm angry at you!"

"If I don't get a cuppa tea this minute, I'll perish!" Francie had already turned up the heat under the quiet kettle.

As Emma entered the kitchen, Francie collapsed into a chair. Her breathing was loud. Her not-at-all-ample chest heaved with each breath. She sobbed once, twice and then came to tears. With one hand she tried in vain to push straggled strands of gray hair back off her face.

"Ah, Emma," she sobbed, "Ya'll never believe it."

Emma sat herself down in the chair next to her friend's. She was very angry. With an adamant shake of her head she vowed, "I'm in no mood to listen to your gossip. And you're right. I won't believe any of your fantasy excuses."

"Well, I'd 'ardly call a corpse a fantasy excuse!" Francie proclaimed.

"A corpse?" Emma was completely taken by surprise.

"Stone cold dead 'e is, and *not* o' natural causes!" Francie put much emphasis on the latter part of her statement.

"Who is dead?"

Francie moved her face closer to Emma's, and with all the dramatic effect she was able to muster, pronounced the victim's name, "Major Arthur Fitzgerald!"

There was a minute of silence, for it took a full minute for Emma to digest what her friend had just told her. When she realized the full implication of what had been said, all Emma could do was to fervently bless herself and say, "Oh, sweet Mother of God."

There was another minute of silence broken only by one or two sobs from Francie.

"You're certain?" Emma dared.

"I am," was the reply.

"*My* Major Fitzgerald?"

"There ain't any other!" Francie snorted.

"You'd better tell me the whole story."

"First ya better pour me a cuppa tea."

The kettle had been whistling for a few seconds now. Emma jumped up to rescue it. She filled two cups and set them on the table. Francie quickly took a sip of the still boiling liquid.

"Now," Emma said resolutely. "Will you please tell me what happened to Major Arthur Fitzgerald?"

After another sip of tea, Francie began her narrative.

"Well, it was a few minutes afore nine o'clock this mornin'. I was just walkin' down past St. Michael Church on me way 'ere, for I knowed ya was full up and would be wantin' me 'elp. Well, din't I see Paddy Finnegan drive 'is milk wagon into the alley behind the Royal to make 'is delivery. And I know 'is missus 'asn't been well, so I cuts across the alley ta be askin' after Paddy's wife's 'ealth. Paddy and me, we chatted for a bit, when Jimmy Rafferty comes out o' the back door o' the Royal. 'E's carryin' out the trash, mind, and cleanin' up the bar from the night afore, Jimmy is."

"Well, the three o' us was just talkin' o' this 'n that when Paddy sees a gent asleep in the corner behind the big trash bin. Paddy, 'e laughs and tells Jimmy there's a big lump o' trash for 'im to throw in the bin. So Jimmy goes over ta the sleepin' gent and gives 'im a shake on the shoulder, thinkin' 'es's drunk, but the gent falls over on 'is side! So Jimmy unbends 'im, but 'e says the man's dead, not drunk, and mortification is startin' ta set in!"

"Then Jimmy tells the both o' us ta get over there and 'ave a look at this man. Well, we did walk over, and when I seed the man's face I screamed me 'ead off! It was 'im—the major! And the side of 'is 'ead was 'alf missin' and covered with blood!"

"Oh, dear Jesus!" Emma Quinn blessed herself again and took a long deep breath before asking, "Then what happened?"

"I'm comin' ta that." Francie was not going to be rushed. She took another sip of her tea before she continued.

"Well, Paddy and Jimmy took me inta the Royal and sat me down wi' a drop o' sherry. Truth be told, it was a bit more than a drop. Anyroad, they rang for the garda, and in a couple a minutes the officers came. Two local boys, they were. Kevin Boyle 'n Brian Curry."

"What did they say?" Emma by now had completely succumbed to her friend's story.

"I'm comin' ta that. Boyle and Curry was all business. They didn't say much o' nothin'." She took time out for another sip of tea.

"They asked us for our statements. O' course, I identified the body…imagine the old major bein' a 'body.' Anyroad, I told 'em about 'is stayin' wi' ya 'n all. I expect they'll be 'ere soon enough ta ask ya what ya know about it."

"What I know about it! What could I know about it?" Emma demanded.

"Well, at least ya know somethin' about the major, which is more than anyone else in Howth knows," Francie stated.

Emma thought for a moment. What <u>did</u> she know about the major? And what would this incident do to her business?

"Oh, God forgive me," she pleaded, "For here I am, wondering if this situation will ruin me for the season when I should be praying for his eternal soul!"

chapter 5

Francie Houlihan did not have a chance to reply to this self-admonishment by her friend, for the words had barely been uttered when there came a firm but polite *rap-rap-rap* on the front door. Both women were a bit startled; however, Emma Quinn quickly rose from her chair, smoothed her apron and walked to the door. Upon opening it, she was greeted by the two local garda, Kevin Boyle and Brian Curry.

"Good afternoon, Mrs. Quinn," said Gard Boyle, tipping his hat. And likewise Gard Curry tipped his cap and said, "Good day to you, ma'am."

"I'm sure I know why you're here," Emma assured them. "Come in, boys."

Both officers entered the house. Knowingly, Gard Curry said, "I take it your friend Mrs. Houlihan has already brought the news."

"She has."

Gard Boyle took from his pocket a small notepad and pen.

"Please, ma'am," he began. "We need some information from you."

Emma nodded her head. "I understand," she said. "Come into my kitchen and have a cup of tea while we talk."

The men followed Mrs. Quinn to her kitchen.

Both young men were brown-haired and sported faces full of freckles. They were still young enough to look innocent and friendly, but Emma remembered when they were both schoolboy rascals. She thought that they had grown up well.

"Francie, get the kettle please," she said.

"Sit down, boys." She motioned them to two empty chairs at the table.

"What do you need to know?"

"First, ma'am, we need to know something about the deceased." This was from Gard Boyle.

"Actually, I know very little about the major."

Gard Boyle continued. "He's been a guest of yours for a number of years, I believe?"

"Eight years, to be exact."

Gard Boyle was writing this in his notepad. Gard Curry continued the questioning.

"Why did he come to Howth?"

Emma Quinn thought about this for a few seconds. She answered, "As far as I know, he came here for a holiday and nothing more. The first year he stayed with me on referral from the Board F'ealte. They called me in mid-May of that year, as I recall, and said that a gentleman from Waterford desired Bed and Breakfast accommodations for two weeks in June and could I take him? Well, I was newly in business and glad to have a guest, even though it was early in the season. So I said, 'certainly.' And on June first he came and stayed until June fifteenth. And every year since it's been the same—someone from the Board calls in mid-May to reserve the room for him. He comes and stays the two weeks, and I don't see him again until the next year."

"What is his address in Waterford?" Gard Boyle asked.

With a shrug of her shoulders and a look of surprise on her face, Emma Quinn admitted that she did not know. The first year that the major visited with her, she had been too timid to ask much about him. In subsequent years, she hadn't bothered, for the major did not invite friendliness. He had been a very private man.

"What did he do when he stayed here?" Gard Curry asked. "You know anything that you can tell us could be an important clue."

"Then you don't know who killed the major?" Emma realized.

"They din't exactly catch anybody in th' act!" Francie's attitude was most unflattering.

"Francie!" Emma admonished. "Pour the tea!"

Now Francie was in a huff.

"If ya ask me, that so-called major is—<u>was</u>—a very suspicious lot! Holiday, me eye! Nearly a recluse 'e was, every time 'e stayed 'ere," she retorted. Nevertheless, she did pour the tea.

Gard Kevin Boyle rather obviously cleared his throat. "Well then, ladies, if we may continue please?"

He turned his attention to Mrs. Quinn.

"Tell me please, just what the major was like."

"All I can tell you is he kept to himself. He was a very private man, God rest his soul. He asked for a little extra service. He didn't become friendly with me or Tommy or any of the guests, ever. He just kept to himself."

"How did he and Tommy get along?" Brian Curry posed this question.

Emma thought carefully about the answer.

"Tommy didn't like him much. He said he was really a Brit trying to pass as Irish. But the only time they ever saw each other was in the late evening, if Tommy happened to be home when the major came in."

"And what kind of extra service did he require?" Curry continued.

"Well, as I said, he was a loner. He didn't like to come to breakfast with the others."

"Tell 'em about 'is queer 'abits!" Francie demanded.

"Oh, Fran!" Mrs. Quinn had to compose herself for a moment.

The gard waited patiently for her to continue.

"The major rose early every morning. He attended seven a.m. Mass at St. Michael Church. I know this, for Father O'Rourke has often mentioned it to me. Then after Mass he spent some time walking, down on the piers,

I believe. Anyway, he always returned here about eight a.m. Then, at eight-thirty a.m., I took his breakfast tray up to him."

"You served him breakfast in his room?" asked Brian Curry. Being a 'local boy,' he was familiar with the B&B custom of serving all the guests together.

"Not really," Emma corrected him. "I took the tray upstairs and set it on the table by his door. I knocked on the door as a signal, you know, then I left."

She again spent a few seconds collecting her thoughts.

"You know, many days the only time I actually saw the major would be around ten-thirty in the morning when Francie and I would be cleaning upstairs."

She shot a castigating glance at her friend.

"He always went out again at ten-thirty, and we'd see him leaving."

Gard Boyle was writing furiously in his notepad. It took him a couple minutes to catch up. Then he asked, "Did you ever find anything suspicious looking when you cleaned his room?"

"What do you mean by suspicious?" Emma was unsure of what she was being asked. Then she added, "Actually, he preferred that I not clean his room during his stay. So I only cleaned it after he left."

Curry considered this statement, and then said, "Never mind. Boyle and I need to have a look-see in that room, if we have your permission."

"Of course," Emma answered.

"Just a couple more questions, then we'll have a look at it." Boyle had his notepad and pen ready again.

"We need to know what the major did during the day," he requested.

With a shrug of her shoulders, Emma Quinn replied that she did not know. But she added, "I know he had his dinner at the Royal every evening at seven o'clock. After dinner he took a brandy to the lounge and sat there with his newspaper and brandy until ten p.m. He always came back here at ten p.m. and went directly to his room. But I can't swear to that, now that I think of it."

"Why do you say that," Boyle asked.

"Because this year I gave him his own key to the house. He was such a steady customer, after all."

chapter 6

"You mean to say that the major could have returned here without you knowing it?"

"Yes. That's why I didn't see him last night. He's been letting himself in with his own key and I really couldn't say what time. But I do know that he leaves the Royal's lounge at ten every evening."

"And how do you know these details?"Boyle questioned.

"From Peggy Conroy."

Both garda men understood, for both being 'local boys,' they knew that Mrs. Conroy was the hostess at the Royal and had been for many years.

"We'll talk to Mrs. Conroy this afternoon,"they agreed.

"Just let me make sure I understand," said Curry. "Between ten-thirty in the morning and seven o'clock in the evening, every day, the major's whereabouts were completely unknown to you."

Emma assured him that his was correct and apologized for her lack of knowledge.

"Now don't be sorry. You've told us a lot more about the deceased than we knew before," they assured her.

"Is that it then?" Emma asked.

"No, not quite. We need a list, the names and addresses of your other guests.

Emma was uncomfortable with this request.

"Do you suspect one of them," she asked.

Gard Boyle comforted her by saying that they suspected no one; it was simply their duty to obtain information.

"In that case," she agreed. "Well, There's Gwillam Morgan. He's a schoolmaster from Wales. Then there's Miss. Jean Blair from Stranraer, Scotland, and her traveling companion, Mrs. Mary MacGregor. She's a widow, also from Stranraer. And last, there are the Murphys—John and Kitty. He's a police officer from Boston…"

"An' she's a bitch!" Frances Houlihan proclaimed.

The garda men snickered in spite of themselves. As professionally, as business-like as possible, Gard Curry informed Mrs. Quinn that they would need to speak to her guests. He asked her cooperation in assembling them at some convenient time, soon.

"That shouldn't be a problem," Emma assured him. "My guests return for afternoon tea at four p.m. Well, most of them, anyway. Gwillam Morgan doesn't always come. But I'll tell everyone today that you must talk to them. Oh, sweet Jesus! I bet they don't even know the major is dead!"

Francie Houlihan cackled at that statement.

"Don't be so sure, me friend. Don't be so sure." And she chortled knowingly.

Emma became even more impatient with her.

"You stop pretending you know something that you don't!" she ordered.

The garda couldn't help but pay attention to this. Kevin Boyle began, "Mrs. Houlihan, please, if you do know something…"

Francie interrupted him slyly. "Ah, well, I'm not sayin' I do, at least nothin' in particular. But I know in 'ere," she pointed a gnarly index finger at her heart, "that those five visitors ain't just right! Ya watch and ya'll see!" She waved the same scrawny finger at the two men.

chapter 7

After this warning, the garda rose from their chairs and asked Emma's permission to see the major's room.

"You'll need the key," she said, taking it from her apron pocket. "Here you are. Francie will show you the way."

As the three left the kitchen and went up the stairs, Francie chattering all the way, Emma took advantage of the solitude to rethink the conversation that had just taken place. She blamed herself for having so little information for the garda.

Tommy might have more information about the major, she thought. She remembered seeing the two men talking outside by the kerb the first evening of the major's arrival this year. But when she'd asked Tommy what they had talked about, he answered tersely, saying, "It's nothing to do with you."

Her quiet time ended, for Frances soon returned.

"They wouldna let me in the room," she complained. "They're takin' snapshots, mind, and collectin' fingerprints. They said they din't need me 'elp."

She was very disappointed.

When the garda had completed their work and were ready to leave Sea View, Emma saw them to the door. They had locked the door of the deceased's room and gave Emma back her key, instructing that no one was to enter that room.

"Of course," she replied.

She couldn't stop herself from asking the men if they had found anything suspicious in there.

They assured her they had not.

Curry asked, "Did you ever find anything out of the way when you cleaned his room?"

"Well, yes, I did," she replied. "You asked that earlier, and I do remember something. Once I found some of those yellow wrappings from an electrical cord, and I couldn't imagine why they were there. I mean, why would he need electric wires at my house?"

Boyle thought for a moment and then asked, "Did he ever carry a curious looking case with him? You know… something too heavy for the size of it. Maybe he carried some kind of recording device?"

"How would I know that?" Emma asked. Then she added, "I never look in anyone's luggage."

Then she offered, "Why don't you come back around four-thirty today? Everyone should be here by then."

Gard Boyle remembered to request that Tommy be present also.

"What time does he get home from work?"

When he saw the look on Emma Quinn's face, he was sorry he'd asked the question.

Her cheeks flushed with embarrassment and she couldn't make eye contact, but her voice asked for no sympathy. She answered, "I never know when to expect him."

They bid her good day, but before she closed the door behind them, she thought of a question.

"If it's not improper to ask," she ventured, "Can you tell me how the poor man met his death?"

Gard Curry hesitated for a moment, and then decided that Emma was truly concerned and could be trusted.

"He was shot, ma'am, at close range. Shot in the head, although the medical examiner will have to make the final statement."

Emma sighed and blessed herself again.

The gard added, "I trust you'll not discuss this with anyone. The inspector prefers to divulge information himself. And then, no more than necessary."

"The inspector?" Emma was puzzled.

"Yes, ma'am. Chief Inspector Desmond Joyce. He's coming to the garda station to take over the investigation."

The importance of this man's name was not lost on Emma Quinn. Why would a killing of a retired Army Major require the attention of the Chief Inspector for County Dublin? She asked the same of the garda.

Neither gard could answer the question.

"I don't know," explained Kevin Boyle. "We called Dublin Castle to report the crime. Your friend Mrs. Houlihan had already identified the body for us. After a moment, our call was put through directly to Desmond Joyce."

"You say he's coming to Howth soon?"

The men confirmed this fact.

"Will he be here at Sea View?"

Gard Curry replied, "We can't say, ma'am. The Chief plays his own game, so to speak. But we'll be back at four-thirty, as we planned. Good day, ma'am."

And with a polite tip of their caps, they departed.

Before Emma stepped back into her foyer, she stood there at her open door, deep in though. The name Desmond Joyce stirred a memory.

She met the Chief Inspector—no, not really met—she was in his presence once, about two years ago. Her woman's club invited him to speak at one of their fundraisers.

She remembered the size of the man. By any standards, he was very large. His voice was incredibly deep. His very manner promoted a feeling of confidence in her. His presence stirred other feelings in her as well.

She remembered catching her breath as he stepped up to the podium. She though she had never seen so manly a man. She wondered what it would feel like to be in his arms, breathing in his male scent. She fantasized about having her breasts pressed tight against his chest.

Because she feared her thoughts would betray her, she was too embarrassed to meet him personally. What if he read her thoughts—sensed her feelings? No, she stayed away from him. And now he was coming to Howth.

Emma shook away the memory, turned and started back into her foyer. She had a shock, however, for she found Francie Houlihan hiding just inside the door.

"Oh, Fran, you nosey biddy!" she scolded.

"Ah, hush!" Fran retorted. "It don't hurt ta be curious," she stated, trying to redeem herself. "I just wish I could be 'ere when ya break the news ta yer guests!"

Chapter 8

Leaving Sea View, Boyle and Curry walked casually back to the garda station. A spotty rain began which caused them to walk a bit faster.

"Holy Jesus!" Boyle exclaimed. "Never in my life did I expect to meet anyone as big as Desmond Joyce." He pulled his coat collar up higher around his neck, as the rain was pelting his back. He began to trot a quicker step.

Curry kept up the pace. He chuckled as he asked his partner, "Just what do you mean by 'big'—his height, his weight or his position on the force?"

They reached the garda station running as fast as possible. They took off their wet coats and hung them on the backs of chairs. They moved the chairs close to the hissing radiator.

"There," said Curry, "That should do the job."

They asked the matronly woman behind the reception desk if the chief inspector had arrived at the station yet.

She stared at them over the top of her glasses, and then challenged, "How long do you propose to leave your coats like that?"

"And what's wrong with them?" Boyle demanded.

"They're cluttering my reception area," the quarrelsome woman averred. "Move them out of here! And no, the chief isn't here yet."

The two chastened men took their wet coats and went to a back room. There they waited for Desmond Joyce.

"What an old witch she is!" stated Curry.

"Bejesus, I hope my wife doesn't turn out to be like her," Boyle said.

"You know what her trouble is!" Curry surmised, and he winked at Boyle like a conspirator!

The chief inspector left Dublin Castle at two p.m. for the hour-long drive to Howth. He was entitled to be driven by a junior officer and to travel in an official vehicle, but today he declined the privilege. Instead, he got into his 1966 apple red Jaguar XKE, started up the engine and pulled into the Dublin traffic. He was looking forward to the drive ahead.

Inspector Joyce remembered being in Howth once before when he delivered a speech to some women's club. Actually, he gave the same speech every time he spoke at a women's club. No one ever seemed aware.

He met so many women in his career—old and young, some plain and some lovely. He never seemed to have had the time to claim one for himself.

Desmond Joyce loved women. He was raised by his parents and his grandmother. He had no siblings. He was such a large baby that his mother 'nearly split in two' delivering him. She refused to have any more babies. His parents argued bitterly about this. They stayed together but were always angry with each other.

But his granny loved him.

He could remember being a young boy, sitting on her cushiony lap, snuggling against her ample bosom and drifting off to sleep. He thought of women in that way... loving, comforting and soft.

He had availed himself of women's other pleasures, although it had been a long time since he'd had that opportunity. He told himself that he was just too busy. In truth, he'd quit trying. He feared that no woman would want such a huge, middle-aged man on top of her. Driving alone in his Jaguar gave him time to consider his life.

He had a professional reputation that was well known and respected. He had a very good income, a great flat and an expensive car, some friends, a bit of a social life. But there was an emptiness inside him. He wanted a wife.

He drove into Howth and headed for the garda station. Pedestrians noticed his red auto. Some eyed it appreciatively. This attention pleased him. He liked being thought of as the guy with the great car. He spent enough time being thought of as the chief inspector.

At the garda station he was greeted by a stout woman at the reception desk. She looked up from the racy romance novel she was reading and stood at attention.

"Good afternoon, sir!" she brayed, excitedly. She actually fluttered her eyelashes at Desmond Joyce. He took a step back from her and was dismayed to see her become coy and flirtatious.

She giggled, "I hope you had a happy little ride here. Did you drive your pretty red car?" She was practically cooing. Her mammoth breasts heaved with each breath.

A Bed and Breakfast Affair

"How can I help you," she asked, but the inference in her manner gave new meaning to her words.

"I want to see Garda Boyle and Curry. Immediately!" He thundered out the words.

She stood there, stunned. Her mouth hung open. Tears spilled from her eyes. She looked like a child, rebuffed for acting silly.

A young female secretary stepped up and rescued the situation. She simply said, "Follow me, sir. The men are waiting for you." She led him down a hall to a conference room and opened the door for him to enter.

Boyle and Curry immediately jumped to attention.

Still peeved at the silly woman at the reception desk, the chief inspector had no time or tolerance for niceties.

"Get your coats on men. Who is driving? You? Get your squad car...I assume there is one?"

"Take me to the crime scene. I'm not walking in this deluge. And you," he said, speaking to the non-driver, "Distract that woman at the desk. I don't want any more attention from her!"

They reached the Royal Hotel in about ten minutes of slow driving. The rain showed no signs of letting up, and the streets were crowded with pedestrians trying to dodge both rain and autos.

"Is the body protected from the rain?" Joyce asked.

"It is, sir—or it should be," answered Curry, the non-driver. "We gave orders to Jimmy Rafferty to cover the area with tarp if the rain started. He's done it to be sure."

"Should or sure?" the chief inspector asked.

"Jimmy's a good man," Curry assured him.

As they spoke, a worried looking man came out of the Royal and approached the squad car. He held a large black umbrella aloft as he opened the car door for the chief.

Desmond Joyce extricated himself from the car slowly and deliberately.

"And you are...?" he asked, addressing the man with the umbrella.

"Jimmy Rafferty, at your service." The man bowed slightly.

"Lead the way. I want to see the body," Joyce directed.

Boyle and Curry followed behind. Reassured to see that the major's body was covered with tarp as they had instructed, they looked at each other and smiled with relief.

The chief lifted the tarp from the major's head while Jimmy Rafferty held his umbrella over Desmond Joyce and the corpse.

The major's face and head were a terrible sight. The right side of the major's head was a bloody pulp, with congealed blood covering a huge cavern in his skull. His right ear was missing as well as part of his right cheek bone and forehead.

The chief inspector motioned for the two garda to come closer. He said, "It looks like someone put a gun right up to his ear and shot him. His killer was either right handed and standing behind him, or left handed and standing face to face with him. Do you agree?"

Boyle questioned, "How could a man with a big gun in his hand get another man to stand still for an exact shot like that?"

"He couldn't," the inspector stated. Then he asked, "So what can we surmise?"

"Well," Boyle answered, "Possibly there were two assailants."

"Or maybe the old major died of fright before he was shot!" Curry ventured.

Boyle continued, "Maybe someone came up behind him and clamped a cloth over his face, you know, with ether or chloroform on it. That would have knocked him out. Then the attacker shot him."

Desmond Joyce rose from kneeling to his full standing height while Boyle adjusted the tarp to cover the victim's face. Joyce directed Curry to summon the coroner.

"He'll be mad as blazes when he finds out the major lay here so long," Curry warned.

"Just tell him I'm in charge of the case."

"Boyle, drive me back to the station. Curry, you wait here for the coroner. Then what are your plans?"

'We're to meet with Mrs. Quinn's guests at Sea View and take their statements," Boyle answered.

"Fine," agreed the inspector. "Tell her I'll see her at ten tomorrow morning."

chapter 9

At four o'clock that afternoon, Emma had already set the table. She was busy in the kitchen, warming scones and filling jam pots with orange marmalade when she heard the Murphys enter the dining room. They were arguing, as usual.

"We've been here for three days, John! I repeat, three days! And I didn't like it in the first place!" Kitty's shrill voice carried well, but she wasn't finished, "And I see you staring at that redhead! You're like a love-sick school boy!"

"I do not stare at her so shut up, Kitty! Keep your voice down or someone will hear you!" he demanded.

"I don't care if someone…" But Kitty stopped in mid-sentence. Emma guessed that someone had joined them in the dining room.

She was right, for as she carried in the tray and tea things, Gwillam Morgan greeted her.

"Oh, Mr. Morgan, I'm glad you're here today," she answered him. She sat the heavy tray down, obviously relieved to be rid of its weight. "Do you suppose the ladies will be in for tea?"

"They're upstairs now. I'm sure they'll be down directly," he answered agreeably.

"Ah, well then, that's good." Emma waited for a minute. She had been trying to think of a way to break the news to her guests, and now that the time was upon her, she still didn't know how to begin.

"Let's just pour some tea, shall we?" she invited. She proceeded to do just that.

Very soon they were joined by the two young women from Scotland. After greetings were exchanged, the ladies seated themselves at the table. Emma poured their tea and passed around the plate of cakes and scones. Gwillam Morgan, Mary MacGregor and Jean Blair were chatting and exchanging pleasantries. John Murphy was trying to appear at ease and attentive to the general conversation.

Only Kitty Murphy seemed not to be a part of the camaraderie. She sat very still, only stirring her tea, anger and resentment evident in her very posture and manner. Emma couldn't help but notice her. Of course, Kitty Murphy had been unhappy since the day she checked into Sea View, but today she seemed especially miserable. Emma wondered why.

Without realizing it, Emma had neither sipped her tea nor eaten a bite. She was studying each guest, one by one, and wondering how to break the news.

Mary MacGregor noticed Emma's preoccupation and asked her directly, "What's on your mind, Mrs. Quinn? You're very quiet today."

All conversation ceased. All eyes turned to Emma.

She said, "I do have something on my mind."

Now that she had begun, she knew how to continue.

"I received some bad news today, and I'm afraid it involves us all."

Curiosity was obvious on each face. Emma continued as simply and calmly as she could.

"This morning Major Fitzgerald was found dead."

Pausing while people expressed their surprise, Emma carefully formulated her next words. "He did not die of natural causes. He was murdered."

Her guests were stunned. They looked at one another, and then all faces turned again to her. Their expressions revealed their shock and confusion.

"Was he killed here?" Mary MacGregor's face blanched as she asked this question.

"No, no, no," Emma assured them all. "His body was found behind the Royal Hotel."

That the Royal was just a couple doors away from Sea View was of concern. The guests were truly discomforted by this information.

Emma watched them all and waited. When everyone was again still, she said, "I'm afraid it's true. The garda have been here already. I talked with them earlier. They're coming back shortly, and they want to talk with each of you."

There was a moment of absolute silence. Then the responses came. They were loud and angry and full of disbelief. The loudest and angriest was Kitty Murphy.

"You mean the police suspect one of us?" was Kitty's hostile question.

The reasonable Jean Blair tried to comfort her. "Mrs. Murphy, I'm sure the garda don't suspect anyone. This is probably just routine police work. Isn't it the same in America, Mr. Murphy?"

"Exactly the same! Quiet down, Kitty!" John Murphy was extremely upset. His fists were clenched and his face was red, but he wasn't looking at his wife. He and Mary MacGregor were locked in each other's sight.

An uncomfortable silence ensued. Once again, thoughts of Desmond Joyce found their way into Emma's mind. She was excited by the thought of him being in Howth. She felt safer, somehow.

But in her heart, she knew the truth. She remembered how she felt in his presence before. She wanted to feel that way again.

chapter 10

There was a knock on the door.

"That'll be the garda," Emma said, and she went to let them in. She returned in a minute with Garda Boyle and Curry.

Gard Boyle began. "Good afternoon, ladies, gentlemen. Please relax. Gard Curry and I need to ask each of you a few simple questions, if you don't mind. May we begin with you, sir?" He directed his attention to Gwillam Morgan.

"Certainly," was the reply. And in response to the questions, he stated that his home was in the town of Rhyll in Flintshire, North Wales, and he was a schoolmaster there. As to his whereabouts on the previous evening, Morgan simply stated, "Dublin."

"Could you be more specific, sir?" asked Gard Curry.

"I'll try, but I'm afraid I didn't pay any special notice to what I was doing or when. I left Howth late morning and lunched at Jury's. Maybe around noon I did some shopping at O'Bieran and Fitzgibbon. I ordered a new coat there. I bought a newspaper and went to St. Stephen's Green to read it. Then I walked up and down some streets, just looking in windows. I had a pint at some small pub and went back to Jury's for dinner. The evening, well, I spent the evening visiting some cabarets, listening to the ballad singing. I got back here at eleven p.m.

"And stayed in all night?" Curry inquired.

Morgan seemed confounded at this. "Certainly," he said. "I never left again 'til after breakfast today."

"Fine, sir," said Boyle, who was busy writing notes in his pad. "Could you tell us the names of the cabarets you visited?"

Morgan shifted in his seat. He seemed a bit hesitant when he answered, "That might be difficult. I think there was one on Baggot Street, and a tiny pub on Henry Street... that was the Goldsmith, I believe. And there was a big, lively place on O'Connell Street, the Tara. But I'm afraid I'd be hard put to prove myself."

"You were alone?" assumed Boyle.

"I was. I spoke to a few people, but no one I knew. I doubt they'd remember me any more than I'd remember them."

"Fine, sir," said Boyle.

Then Boyle turned his attention to Jean Blair, who readily answered his questions. She and Mary MacGregor established that, shortly after breakfast, they had driven south to County Wicklow. There they had explored the ruins of St. Kevin's Monastery and the Vale of Glendalough.

Here Boyle interrupted, smiling pleasantly and said, "A beautiful spot, that is. Did you examine the old tombstones there?"

Mary MacGregor answered, saying, "You're absolutely right. The area has both beauty and fascination." She added, "We went to the Avoca hand weavers and watched them at their work, too."

Jean Blair agreed. "We loved Glendaloch. We learned a lot about the monk's tower. What a frightening time the ninth century must have been!"

The ladies were smiling and relaxed. They said that after this sightseeing, they returned to Sea View in time for tea, spent some time resting in their room and then went to dinner at the Abbey Tavern. Yes, they had stayed for the ballad singing. No, their story could not be corroborated by anyone, except perhaps the waitress would remember them.

"Although," Mary MacGregor added impishly, "John and Kitty were also at the Abbey last evening."

"So the four of you all went to the Abbey last night," commented Gard Curry. "Did you have a party then?"

"We did _not_ all go together, officer," Kitty Murphy reacted predictably. "My husband and I dined alone. We were not with these two ladies at any time!" She was as catty as her name.

"I see," replied Gard Curry, concealing his bemused grin. "Could you two please, briefly tell me of your whereabouts yesterday?"

"Be glad to oblige," offered John Murphy expansively. "Actually, the wife and I were in Dublin, too, although we didn't run into Morgan there. We just ate lunch somewhere— don't remember the name of the place, one of those 'double egg, double sausage' grills. We walked around, took some photos, bought some souvenirs for friends at home."

"I can show you the merchandise, and I have every sales receipt," Kitty assured him.

"I'm sure you do," Curry smiled indulgently. Then he scanned John and Kitty's faces and asked, "What time did you get in here last night?"

"We were in at ten-thirty p.m., and stayed in all night," John Murphy stated.

Curry looked just as intently at the two Scots women as he had the Murphys. "And you ladies," he asked. "What time did you get in?"

Jean Blair told him, "We came through the door just a few minutes before ten-thirty p.m."

Mary MacGregor added that it was preposterous to think that she or Jean would leave the house again during the night. "And just why are you asking that?" she countered.

"Because we want to do a thorough job," Curry said, a bit of steel in his voice.

"And we have a very important 'higher-up' to answer to," added Boyle.

Chapter 11

Mary's statement was challenged, albeit politely, by Emma Quinn. Naively, she stated, "Mrs. MacGregor, maybe you've forgotten. You and Mr. Murphy were both standing outside the door when I went to lock up last night."

Boyle looked squarely at John Murphy, and then at Mary MacGregor. He asked of Mrs. Quinn, "What time was that?"

Emma now wished she hadn't spoken, but she knew she had to answer the officer. "It was a few minutes before eleven, I think."

And here Gwillam Morgan interjected, "You're right. Remember? I'd just parked my car, and I saw you talking to them. I sprinted up to the porch and came in with Mary and John."

Kitty Murphy turned to face her husband. She didn't try to control her anger, hissing, "You lying louse!"

John Murphy responded in kind. "Oh, shut up!" he demanded.

Then, addressing Boyle, he emphatically stated, "I just stepped out for a cigarette."

Kitty wasn't about to be quiet. "And why would you do that when you constantly smoke in our room?" she accused.

"Maybe I wanted to get away from you!" he thundered.

"And maybe you wanted to be alone with that woman!" she seethed.

Gard Curry stood up from his chair and demanded the argument cease. Quiet was restored, but there was certainly no peace. The atmosphere was tense. Kitty was still angry, John resentful. Jean Blair sat studying her tea. Gwillam Morgan seemed to wish he were anywhere but in that dining room.

Mary MacGregor, however, sat erect, shoulders squared, her expression controlled, staring at Kitty Murphy. Without shifting her gaze, she said sarcastically, "If I may—I went outside to look at the stars. I'd no idea that Mr. Murphy would be there."

Turning her attention to the garda, she added, "I didn't consider that leaving the premises."

Gard Boyle closed his notepad. "I think everyone needs to cool off," he said. "Inspector Joyce will be here tomorrow, and he won't stand for this kind of nonsense."

Boyle continued, "The inspector will want to talk with you, Mrs. Quinn, and with Tommy. I take it Tommy couldn't be here today."

Emma nodded yes, and was grateful for Boyle's tact.

Boyle added, "Inspector Joyce asks that all of you plan to stay here for the next few days."

"I would like to know why!" demanded Kitty Murphy. "Are we suspects?"

"Kitty! For heaven's sake, be reasonable," her husband implored. "These men aren't in charge of the investigation. They're just following orders."

Mary MacGregor stood up from her chair. "Pardon me, gentlemen," she said, addressing the garda. "Did you say Inspector Joyce?"

"Yes, miss," replied Curry.

"Is that Chief Inspector Desmond Joyce?" the widow asked, her voice slightly cautious.

"Why do you ask, miss?" the gard returned question for question.

Mary flushed slightly. "He's been mentioned often in the Stranraer newspapers. I'm surprised that a man of his reputation would concern himself personally with this case."

Emma Quinn hurried to appease her. "I thought he was only involved in matters of internal government investigation," she offered, hoping her reddening face wasn't betraying her earlier thoughts about him.

"He is, ma'am," said Boyle. "He's not just an ordinary investigator," he added.

With that, both garda tipped their hats and bid farewell to all present.

The garda let themselves out of the house, for Emma Quinn and her guests were too stunned to move. The impact of what they'd just heard was making itself felt. The effect was overwhelming.

John Murphy stood up facing Mary MacGregor. He quickly looked around at everyone and smiled, saying, "Well, Mrs. Quinn, I guess we'll all be your guests for a few more days." He laughed nervously, and then addressed his wife. "Come on, Kitty. Let's go for a ride or something."

The Murphys left and others soon followed. Emma Quinn was left sitting alone at her dining room table, wondering what was happening to her life.

Chapter 12

Emma clearly remembered John and Mary standing just outside Sea View's door, talking on the previous night. She saw them shortly before eleven o'clock. She wondered why they remained out of doors on such a cold, damp evening and intended to invite them in.

When Emma went to the door, she found it ajar by two or three inches. She could hear their voices and stayed for a few minutes to listen.

John Murphy asked Mary, "Did you have any trouble getting a reservation here?"

"None at all," she answered. "The Board said they are used to people asking for a particular B&B. They were happy to accommodate Jean and me."

"Have you known Jean long?" John asked.

"Just a couple years, but we are good friends."

"I guess you've told her all about yourself," he ventured.

"No, not totally," Mary replied.

They both were quiet for a few moments. Then Mary continued, "I met her at the bank soon after my husband died. I was learning the new job and still in mourning for him. He was all I ever talked about."

"Naturally," he said, but turned his gaze from her to the night sky. He lit a cigarette and offered one to Mary. They smoked their Woodbines silently for a while. He commented that cigarettes were expensive in Ireland, compared to Boston.

She commented that they cost about as much here as they did in Stranraer.

Suddenly she asked, "How long have you and Kitty been married?"

He snickered, and then said, "Would you believe fourteen years?" He snickered again.

"Children?" she ventured.

"No, thank God," he replied, still chuckling. God knew better than to send us babies. Kitty is our baby, herself."

At this, Mary was noncommittal.

"You?" he asked. "Kids?"

She shook her head no. "We thought we still had lots of time to have children. Then he got sick—leukemia. And was dead six months later. I wouldn't know what to do with a child now. Really, it's for the best."

"We might not be here, either of us, if there'd been children," he observed.

"What will you do when this holiday is over," he asked, turning to look directly at her.

"I don't know," she said, thoughtfully. "I may just go back to my life. If this goes well. If it doesn't go well—I don't know. And you? What will you do?"

He shrugged his shoulders as he exhaled a long stream of smoke. "I have to stay with the Boston P.D. for two more years. That'll give me my twenty. After that, I don't know."

He was quiet for a bit, and then, as though thinking aloud, he said, "I dare not divorce Kitty. She'd get half of everything—everything I worked for and paid for."

He extinguished his cigarette, and then asked, "Where will you go when you leave Howth?"

She smiled a bit, and then answered, "It really doesn't matter to me. I told Jean that the rest of the vacation is hers to plan. Howth is the only spot I insisted on."

John lit another Woodbine and was about to offer one to Mary when a black Fiat pulled up to the kerb in front of the house. Out of the auto jumped Gwillam Morgan.

Gwillam hurried to the door of Sea View, delighted to see Mary MacGregor there. Then he noticed John Murphy, and the expression on his face clouded.

Morgan asked, "Why are you two out here so late?"

He tried to smile, but his suspicion was obvious.

Mary smiled at him as though his surprise appearance pleased her. Ignoring his question, she asked him, "And just where have you been all evening?" She smiled all the while.

Morgan relaxed under her gaze. "I've just spent the day in Dublin," he stated. His infatuation with her was obvious.

John Murphy was about to leave the two others when the door opened from the inside and Emma Quinn greeted them.

"I'm about to lock up now," she said pleasantly. "Would you mind coming in for the night?" She was acting the part of the gracious hostess. She had listened to their conversation, but she was certain they were unaware of her presence. She felt no guilt as she stepped aside and allowed her three guests to enter. She was still absorbed by what she had heard. She thought that the conversation had been quite personal for two people who had just met two days ago. And Gwillam Morgan really did seem like a schoolboy in love.

The guests went upstairs, and Emma was about to lock the door when she heard someone cussing outside. She opened the door. There was Tommy, her husband, drunk beyond belief.

Tommy was spewing damnations upon everyone he could think of—the English, the priest, his father. Between cusses he blubbered out a raucous song, "Oh me name it is Sam Hall, Sam Hall..."

Emma quieted him and fairly pushed him into the parlor to the sofa. He collapsed onto it and was instantly asleep. She went into her kitchen and sat a while at her table.

She gave no thought to Tommy. His drunkenness was something she was used to. Instead, she remembered the conversation she had overheard. John and Mary had spoken politely to each other, as two strangers might. But it seemed that their encounter wasn't by accident; it seemed that their ten-thirty p.m. meeting was prearranged.

All this had happened the night before, and Major Fitzgerald had been found dead this morning. The whole situation was more than she could fathom.

Emma shook herself back to the present. Her dining table was still laid with tea dishes and leftover scones. She realized that her guests were leaving the room, talking among themselves.

She remembered the garda saying as they left, "Inspector Joyce will be here around ten tomorrow morning." She gasped when she heard that, and for a second she panicked.

"Do I have to be here?" she asked, and immediately, she felt stupid.

"Now, don't be afraid of the chief," Gard Boyle answered. "He seems to be all business."

chapter 13

At six-thirty a.m., Wednesday, June sixth, Father O'Rourke approached the altar of St. Michael Roman Catholic Church for the first Mass of the day. At seventy-six years, Patrick Joseph O'Rourke had passed the age when priests normally retire. Each year on the anniversary of his birthday, the Bishop of Dublin offered him the opportunity to end his active ministry. Each year, Father O'Rourke politely requested to stay a bit longer, and the bishop granted his request.

To the pastor, known in his youth as P.J., retirement would be the equivalent of sitting around listening to his arteries harden. He had no desire to do that.

He and St. Michael Church were about the same age. They both suffered from creaks, groans and excess wind, but to Father O'Rourke, they both were still able to be of service.

This morning the usual regular parishioners were there, a handful of elderly, local people. The priest looked back to where Major Arthur Fitzgerald usually sat, even though he knew the major wouldn't be there. Yesterday morning Father O'Rourke had administered the Last Rites of the Church to the deceased major, and a terrible shock it had been.

The priest had given the final sacrament of the Church to many departing and departed souls, but it had been many, many years since he had been called to bless the soul of a man who had been murdered. The first time had been twenty-five years ago; the second time, yesterday.

As the opening prayer commenced, Father O'Rourke noticed a stranger enter the chapel, quickly genuflect and take a seat in a side pew. The stranger was a large man both in height and girth. Although the priest knew that this man was not a local resident, there was something vaguely familiar about him. Throughout the mass the priest gave an occasional thought to the identity of this stranger, but the elderly cleric proceeded unerringly through the prayers, a brief homily, and then the Eucharist. At the end of the Mass, the priest walked down the aisle to the outer door of the church and shook hands with his parishioners, one by one, as they left. The stranger waited, letting all the others precede him. Finally, he approached the priest.

"Good morning to you, Father," the big man said. "I wonder if I might have a few minutes of your time." The man's voice was deep and resonant, befitting the size of his body. His handshake was firm but formal.

"Certainly, certainly," answered Father O'Rourke. "Do I know you?" he asked, obviously studying the stranger's face.

"We've not met previously," was the response. "Let me introduce myself."

The man reached inside the left breast pocket of his coat and took out a small leather case. He opened the case, revealing a silver metal badge. "I'm Inspector Desmond Joyce of the Garda Siochana."

A flicker of recognition passed over the priest's face. "Of course, of course. That's why I thought you looked familiar."

"We've never met," said the inspector, with no trace of doubt in his voice.

"I know, sir, I know. But I've seen your picture in the paper many, many times. Surely you're here to investigate that terrible, terrible business yesterday."

The reply was simply a quick nod of the head. Chief Inspector Desmond Joyce had an international reputation, one that was absolutely unblemished according to every article ever written about him. In these articles, he had been described as thorough, comprehensive and possessing an innate instinct for investigation. He had also been described by some newspaper reporters as elusive and nearly uncommunicative. That he was a man of few, but well-chosen words, seemed obvious to Father O'Rourke.

"Tell me what you know about the deceased," required the inspector.

So Father O'Rourke told his simple story of Major Arthur Fitzgerald who appeared in Howth every year on the first day of June, stayed two weeks and attended Mass at seven a.m. every day of his visit.

Chief Inspector Desmond Joyce did not take notes as the priest talked, for years of experience had taught him to listen closely and carefully to people giving information. When the priest finished, the inspector nodded and said, "Yes, I see." He was quiet for a few minutes, and then asked, "Father, did you ever see the major at any other time of the day?"

"No sir, no sir. Only every morning at Mass, as I said."

The inspector did not reply. He and the priest stepped outside the church, and the inspector turned his sight to the village and the streets near the church. He noted how the property belonging to St. Michael Church formed a V, with Thormanby Road on the right and Doctors Road on the left. Both roads joined in front of the church and formed the High Street, which proceeded for eight long blocks down a hill and led out to a fishing pier.

On the Thormanby Road side of the church stood the Royal Howth Hotel, the site of yesterday's murder. Two doors down on the High Street from the Royal was a sign, identifying a Bed and Breakfast establishment named Sea View. This, Desmond Joyce already knew, was where the deceased major had stayed every year during his holiday. The inspector knew about Arthur Fitzgerald. He could only guess why the major had been killed. He just didn't know who did it.

chapter 14

Howth had the picturesque quaintness common to Irish villages: homes built into a hillside with barely enough room to walk out the back door; homes and shops with stucco exteriors, some painted pink or blue, but most left the natural clay-gray color. Most structures fairly abutted the pedestrian sidewalk. However, those fortunate enough to sit back a bit had front gardens, for the Irish loved their flowers.

Ireland's year-round moderate temperatures and the moist sea air fostered glorious flowers. Houses that had no room for a garden had a flower box, overflowing with blooms, at every window.

Not a likely spot for a murder, Inspector Joyce thought.

Father O'Rourke interrupted the inspector's thinking. "Would there be anything else, sir? Anything else?"

Desmond Joyce turned his attention back to the priest. Father O'Rourke was a small, frail, elderly man. Wisps of hair still grew from his pate, but the man's hair had largely gone the way of his youth. The inspector knew him to be nearly eighty years old, about ten years older than the deceased.

"Anything else, sir?" Father O'Rourke repeated.

"One more question, Father. Had you known the deceased before he began making his yearly pilgrimage to Howth?"

The little man was obviously surprised by this question. "By my faith, sir! I did know Arthur Fitzgerald some years ago, I did. How did you know that?"

The faintest trace of a smile creased the face of the big, solemn detective.

"How long ago did you know him?" he asked.

The elderly priest ran a thin, trembling hand through his sparse, white hair. "Let me see now, let me see. Ah, I recall now. It was during the war, WWII of course. Must be twenty-four or twenty-five years ago, at least. He wasn't a major then. No, no, he was a sergeant as I recall. I didn't know him well, oh no. I was the new vicar here at St. Michael. He was here recovering from war injuries, first in hospital, then at a convalescent home. Of course, it's the name I remember. We were both a lot younger then." The priest chuckled at his own agedness.

Inspector Joyce waited quietly while the priest enjoyed his laugh. Then he summed up what Father O'Rourke had told him.

"Approximately twenty-five years ago you were a new priest here. Arthur Fitzgerald was a sergeant of the British Army, staying here to recuperate. You were not friends, merely acquaintances. He left. You remained here. You did not see him again until eight years ago this month, when he appeared at morning Mass. You probably acknowledged him as a stranger and introduced yourself. You recognized his name. You again did not become friends, but simply renewed acquaintance every June."

Father O'Rourke nodded his head energetically throughout Inspector Joyce's summation. The inspector was lost in thought for a moment. Then he asked, "Is it your habit to be here at the door after every Mass?"

"It is, sir, it is." Why do you ask?"

Desmond Joyce did not answer the Father's question. Instead, he posed, "Do you watch your parishioners leave the church property?"

"Sometimes I do, sir."

"Yesterday morning, was Arthur Fitzgerald here for Mass?"

"He was, sir. Yes, he was."

"Did you watch him leave?"

"I did."

"Did he walk away as usual?"

"He did not, sir. He did not," and the priest chuckled again. "You are amazing, sir. How did you know he got a lift?"

The inspector merely said, "Tell me what happened."

"Well, sir, he had just crossed over Doctors Road. Yes he had, when a small brown Ford drove up from the pier and pulled up to the kerb beside him. Right beside him! A man jumped out and took the major into the Ford. And the auto left. It just left."

"Did they struggle?"

The priest hesitated for a moment, and then said, "No struggle, no. The man raised his voice, shouted at the major and pushed him a bit, yes he did. But the major didn't struggle."

"Did you hear what the man said?"

"No, no, sir. I did not."

"Can you describe this man?"

Now the priest scratched his chin as he thought about his answer.

"He was terribly thin, yes thin, and quick in his movements. Thin and quick. But I can't be sure who he was, sir. I can't be sure. He had those jerky, quick movements that the drink gives you. Just watch Tommy Quinn and you'll see what I mean. But it couldn't have been Tommy, for he would've been at work, and he doesn't have a car. Anyway, 'twas very foggy. I can't be sure at all. No, not at all."

The inspector continued. "This man—was he alone? Was he the driver?"

Father O'Rourke had a sudden realization. "There had to be another man. Yes, there had to be. This man put the major into the back seat of the car and got in beside him!"

"And which direction did the car go?"

The priest shrugged his shoulders. "I presume it left Howth on Doctors Road. I can't be sure, sir."

Chapter 15

Chief Inspector Desmond Joyce left Father O'Rourke standing at the open door of St. Michael Church. He walked slowly down the High Street, noticing that the tiny shops and stores were still closed. However, many housewives were up and about already. They seemed to be engaged in an early morning ritual of washing windows, sweeping steps and polishing doorknobs. Some brave women were hanging out wash, although the sky was overcast and rain seem imminent.

The inspector arrived at the pier after about ten minutes of slow walking. He tried to estimate the pace of a man about seventy years old. He strolled about a quarter of the way out onto the pier. The fishing boats were long ago out to sea, but here and there were individual fisherman, seated on the pier and casting their lines out into the immediate waters. The inspector considered for a moment whether or not to question some of them as to their possible acquaintance with the deceased major. He decided, however, that Garda Boyle and Curry could do that questioning, for by now, nearly eight a.m., Desmond Joyce was hungry. By the size of him, it was obvious the inspector was a man who didn't often miss a meal. He decided the logical place to breakfast was the Royal Howth Hotel.

At the Royal he was directed to the dining room by a young, freckle-faced, sleepy-eyed girl. He asked the girl if Mrs. Peggy Conroy was in at that hour. The girl informed him that Mrs. Conroy did not begin her workday until four p.m. He decided to visit the woman later at her home. In the meantime, he would eat his breakfast. He ordered his meal of double eggs, double sausage, broiled tomatoes, brown soda bread and tea. He ate his breakfast leisurely, but did not order a second pot of tea. He had no time for that luxury. Instead, he paid the check and walked to the address of Mrs. Conroy.

The information that Inspector Joyce had received from the two local garda officers about the habits of the deceased had been sketchy, at best. He hoped that Peggy Conroy would be able to tell him more than she had told Boyle and Curry. Sometimes it just took a bit of experience to know what questions to ask. He found her home easily.

Mrs. Conroy answered her door promptly. She was a stylish, still attractive woman, probably in her late forties. Inspector Joyce introduced himself and was welcomed into her home.

If Peggy Conroy was surprised by his visit, she did not seem it. She admitted that the young receptionist at the Royal had phoned earlier that morning, informing her of the rather imposing man who was asking about her. Mrs. Conroy assumed that the man was a garda official. She hadn't expected the official would be Desmond Joyce, but she had met many important people at the Royal Howth Hotel. She took this encounter in her stride. They discussed the deceased major and, in particular, his habit of dining at the Royal every evening.

It did seem that she knew the major's evening habits well. However, she scarcely knew the man himself at all. She could only repeat to the inspector what she had already told Kevin Boyle and Brian Curry, that the major came in to dinner every evening at seven p.m., and he dined alone. After dinner he took a glass of brandy to the lounge and read his paper until about ten p.m., at which time he left. He was never joined by anyone.

Desmond Joyce listened to Peggy Conroy's testimony without comment. When she finished, he asked her one question. "Did anyone ever make an overture to the major, either friendly or unfriendly?"

"An overture? I don't quite know what you mean, inspector." Peggy flustered.

Desmond Joyce explained carefully. "Did anyone ask questions about him, invite him to join them? Did anyone make any derogatory statements about him?"

Peggy Conroy seemed almost shocked to remember something. "A couple of nights ago some people did ask about him. I hardly gave it a thought. It didn't seem like anything."

"Please tell me about it," the inspector requested.

"Well, there were three people eating dinner together. It was Saturday evening, I believe. Yes, Saturday. Anyway, these three took a table. They asked me if I thought that the elderly gentleman eating alone would like to join them. I said I was sure that Major Fitzgerald preferred to dine alone, as this was always his custom. And that was all."

Inspector Joyce looked intently at Peggy Conroy. "I want you to think carefully," he said. "Did you indeed state the major's name?"

Peggy Conroy became visibly worried. "I'm sure I did, sir," she said.

Then, with embarrassment, she added, "I believe I mentioned something about him taking his brandy to the lounge afterwards, too."

The inspector was sure she had.

Then she had a terrible thought. "Do you think they were the killers?" she asked.

Inspector Joyce attempted to assuage her guilt. "At this time, ma'am, I have no reason to suspect anyone. Please don't upset yourself. One more question, please. Can you describe those three people?"

"Oh, certainly, sir! They're staying here in Howth with Mrs. Quinn. There's an American couple. He's a big man with red hair. She's a blonde—bleached, I believe—and wears lots of makeup. The third person was a Welshman, a tall, thin, fair-haired Welshman. But I'm afraid I'd not be able to recall their names."

Inspector Joyce smiled his faint, tolerant smile.

"You've been a great help, ma'am," he said.

As he rose to leave, he turned and looked at Mrs. Conroy.

"Please do not discuss this with anyone," he directed. And he bid her good day.

chapter 16

A sprinkle of rain was falling as Inspector Joyce left the home of Peggy Conroy and walked toward Sea View. But a man who has spent all of his near-fifty years in Ireland regards a fine drizzle as a minor annoyance, nothing more.

As he approached Sea View, he observed the neat, orderly garden in front of the house. A very attractive little garden it was, with lilacs fragrantly in bloom and a number of rhododendrons with flowers of white, lavender and red. A cobblestone walk, neatly swept, led from the kerb to the front door of the white stucco house, and deftly lined along both sides of the walk was a column of tulips, tall and erect. The grass was well clipped and droplets of rain glistened on buds and flowers.

The inspector paused and let his senses fill with the offerings of this little garden. Its harmony pleased him. He had always found a kind of peace in orderliness. The spectrum of colors and the headiness of the fragrances were delightful to him. Desmond Joyce, a man of method, deduction and calculation, a man whose profession involved him in the pettiness, the corruption and the evil in people, realized at moments like this how little beauty there was in his life.

This garden is the work of someone who loves beauty and order, he thought. *I wonder if Mrs. Quinn is the gardener.*

Inside Sea View, Emma Quinn stood at her parlor window. Francie Houlihan was there too, seated on the davenport and chattering on about some nonsense. Emma wasn't listening to her friend. Instead, she was studying the man standing in her garden.

She watched as he let himself become absorbed in her garden. He stood near a lilac bush and pulled a blossom closer to him. He fairly drank in its aroma. Then he stepped closer to her thorny bush of Seven Sisters roses. He bent a little to smell the roses but avoided touching them. Emma suspected that he'd had experience with jagged thorns.

She knew who he was, of course. She'd seen him on the telly being interviewed about his investigations. She remembered how powerful a presence he was and how drawn to him she felt. She knew she would blush when they met face to face.

Emma went to the door and opened it for him while he was still absorbed by the flowers.

"Come in out of the rain," she said, before he had the chance to say anything.

He stepped inside the door.

"Mrs. Quinn?" he asked.

"I am she," Emma answered, and offered him her hand.

"I was expecting you, sir."

She wondered why she wanted to say 'welcome home.' She began to tremble. Her heart pounded within her throat. Her voice betrayed the stirring she felt. Every fiber of her being was responding to this man.

Emma thought she had never before seen so large a man. Well over six feet tall he was, to be sure, and he could easily have weighed 20 stone. His ears were large, though flat against his head, and his nose was large and prominent. He had an oversized, bushy brown moustache that almost obscured his upper lip. But his eyes were warm and smiling, beautiful really. She couldn't look away from him.

As for Desmond Joyce, the man was acutely aware of the gentle hand he was holding. What he observed in the person of Mrs. Emma Quinn was a tall, graceful woman with a sweet smile and warm, soft hands.

What a lovely woman, he thought. He thoroughly approved of her fair Irish skin and her wavy dark hair. He said nothing, but his eyes searched hers as if to say, *"I've found you at last."* For a moment they stood absolutely still, joined by eyes and hands.

"I'm forgetting my manners, inspector," she said abruptly. She quickly withdrew her hand from his, while her face blushed, a girlish pink. "Come into my kitchen and we'll talk."

She led the way, talking a little nervously as they walked. "Gard Boyle and Gard Curry told me you'd be here. Do you want to talk to my guests now?"

"I'd prefer to talk to you alone," he responded. The huskiness of his voice surprised him.

When they reached the kitchen, they found Francie Houlihan trying to set out cups and saucers for tea, but she was so excited! Her hands were flying everywhere, trying in vain to center her apron, pull the wrinkles out of her dress and set the table, all at once. She greeted the inspector, "As soon as I heered yer voice, I knowed it was you. I saw ya on the telly just a couple a months ago, and I says ta meself then, if I ever heered yer voice again, I'd know it was you!"

Emma sighed softly. Knowing that it was useless to ask Francie to act with more composure, she simply introduced her to the inspector.

"This is my friend, Frances Houlihan," she explained.

"I identified the body!" the woman blurted out.

Desmond Joyce acknowledged the introduction with a polite smile. He said, "Gard Boyle told me of your helpfulness. If I need to speak to you further, I will send word to you. At present, I need to speak to Mrs. Quinn privately. Good day, Mrs. Houlihan. Nice meeting you, I'm sure."

Frances Houlihan was summarily dismissed! Emma turned away so her friend wouldn't see her grin, but Francie left immediately, in a state of bewilderment.

chapter 17

"May we sit down, Mrs. Quinn?" Inspector Joyce's question sounded like a polite command, but his eyes were warm and smiling.

"Please, sir, sit. I'm forgetting my manners again."

Emma poured them each a cup of tea and then took a seat across the table from the huge man.

Desmond Joyce spent a few moments looking about Emma's kitchen. He could detect the delicious aroma of fresh bread baking.

"You have an Aga cooker," he commented.

"I do," she smiled. "It's my one luxury."

"You're a great cook, aren't you?" he asked.

Still smiling, she answered, "The Aga and I do pretty well together."

He reached over and touched some fresh roses that were beautifully arranged in a blue crockery vase, sitting on the center of the table.

"Did you pick these this morning?" he asked.

She had, she said, adding, "Roses are my passion."

Desmond Joyce remembered that he had an interview to conduct. He was already very favorably impressed with Emma Quinn's composure and gentleness. He wanted to know her much better. He said, "You caught me admiring the garden. Is that your work?"

She was pleased by his attention and smiled in return. "It is my garden. Thank you. I love growing flowers."

She hesitated a moment and then confessed, "Sometimes I just stand there in the middle of it so I can breathe in all the scents."

He returned her smile. "It must be a lot of work?" he asked gently.

She responded softly, still smiling, "It's work I love."

Desmond Joyce was aware that he admired this woman. He thought that if she proved to be as sensitive to people as she was about her garden, she might have some useful information about this murder case. And she was lovely to look at. He would need to spend a lot of time with her, and the idea pleased him well.

Thank God she's not a bit like that addle-brained friend of hers, he thought.

He already knew a little bit about her from the local garda. She had a husband, he'd been told.

I wish she weren't married, he thought, and surprised himself with the revelation. Feelings weren't something he was comfortable with. Still, this woman stirred something in him. He wondered what sort of man she'd married.

He forced himself back to reality. Daydreaming and fanaticizing were luxuries he couldn't afford now. He had a murder to solve. And this woman, no matter how lovely, was someone he had to question.

He began abruptly. "The local garda have already given me your statement. I've familiarized myself with the details, especially those pertaining to the habits of the deceased. I have some questions about him, if you don't mind."

"Certainly, inspector." She was both flattered and embarrassed by his intent gaze.

"Did the major ever refer to his initial stay in Howth, some twenty-five years ago?"

Emma's surprise was immediate. "Why, no, sir! I didn't know he'd been here before!"

"He was a patient in the hospital, suffering with some sort of war injuries—World War II, of course. He never mentioned why he came back to Howth eight years ago?"

"He did not, sir. If I may…"

The inspector nodded his consent.

"The major wasn't a man you could ask personal questions of. He came and went regularly without ever getting to know us, or we him."

The inspector waited, for Emma was obviously considering something.

"Do you think there's a connection between his stay here twenty-five years ago and his return eight years ago?' she ventured.

"Possibly."

He paused a few seconds while he noticed that she had very lovely blue eyes. He cleared his throat and brought his thoughts back to the reason for his visit.

"Mrs. Quinn, how long have you lived in Howth?"

"Tommy and I moved here as newlyweds, twenty years ago. Both born and raised in Contarf, we were."

"Father O'Rourke was already the pastor at St. Michael when you moved here?"

"He was. In fact, he just celebrated his twenty-fifth anniversary here."

Desmond Joyce made no immediate reply.

Then a question occurred to Emma. "How did you know the major had been here before?"

He smiled at her innocence, but said only, "I knew. Also, Father O'Rourke knew him then. I've already spoken with the pastor. He told me that he tried to minister to the boys who were injured in the war."

Emma was puzzled. "It's odd that he never mentioned it to me. Every year, we discussed the major's return."

"Is it possible that the good Father's mental faculties are not what they once were?" the inspector suggested gently.

Emma considered that possibility.

"You might say that of late, sir. But eight years ago there was nothing wrong with him. He hasn't been well recently. He had a serious operation a year ago. But until a year or so ago, he was that sharp."

Then another thought occurred to Emma.

"Pardon me, sir…"

The inspector motioned for her to continue.

"Well, I was just wondering about something. How is it that a British soldier was in an Irish hospital? Why wasn't he in England? And how could Father O'Rourke remember him after all these years?"

"I wondered that, too."

Silently, Desmond Joyce found himself admiring something else about Mrs. Quinn—her neat, orderly thinking. He had already planned to visit the aged pastor again, very soon.

In answer to her question, he said, "There were some British soldiers in hospitals here. Remember, most all British medical staff and supplies were sent to the front. I believe there were German fliers here, too. And why did the padre remember Arthur Fitzgerald? I don't have the answer to that."

"But, let's not spend any more time talking about the Father," he said. "Let's consider your other guests for a minute. Have any of them ever been here before?"

Emma felt some reluctance to discuss her guests. She hesitated before answering. Desmond Joyce reassured her by saying, "This is very important, Mrs. Quinn."

She knew she had no choice but to answer his question.

"Well, yes, I believe I heard Mr. Morgan say that he'd been to Howth many times. This is the first time he's stayed with me."

"So you hadn't met him prior to his coming to stay at Sea View."

"No, sir. Never before."

"Why does he come to Howth?"

"Actually, it's Dublin that he likes. He spends most of his days and evenings there. I guess that Howth is quieter for him to spend the night in."

"When did Mr. Morgan arrive here?" the inspector continued.

"It was last Saturday, June second. In fact, he arrived at the same time as the Murphys."

"Do you think there's a possibility that they knew each other previously?"

He was treating her gently, asking questions and talking to her in a warm, almost intimate manner.

Emma answered with certainty. "No, I'm sure not. We all introduced ourselves. Straight away, John Murphy insisted that Morgan come to dinner with him and his wife. Mr. Morgan was that surprised, I'll tell you. Mrs. Murphy was staring daggers at her husband when he did that, but it didn't faze him. He made a party of it."

"They had dinner at the Royal Howth Hotel?" the inspector asked, confirming Peggy Conroy's statement.

"I believe they did," Emma replied.

Desmond Joyce waited a moment, as though collecting his thoughts. Then he asked, "How did Morgan make his reservation with you?"

A Bed and Breakfast Affair

"He didn't. He just knocked at the door and asked if I had any accommodations. Luckily enough, I had the small, single room available."

"I see. And the Murphys? Did they have a reservation?"

"They did, indeed. They wrote me about three months ago, saying some friends of theirs had stayed with me a couple of years ago—the Burkes, they were. And the Burkes had recommended Sea View to them."

Again the inspector had to collect his thoughts. Then he asked, "Do you remember the Burkes?"

Emma nodded, "I do, sir. And I'll tell you why. That was a very lean summer. It was the year of the postal strike, 1965. I had very few guests that particular year."

The inspector leaned over the table, just a little closer to Emma Quinn's face. "Tell me, can you remember if the Burkes were here at the same time as Major Fitzgerald?"

Emma answered gravely, "I know they were. They were my only guests in June of that year."

Their unspoken thoughts were identical...*The Burkes knew of the existence and peculiar habits of a strange old man by the name of Arthur Fitzgerald. Did the Burkes tell their friends, the Murphys, about this old man? And if so, why?*

Emma Quinn was the first to speak. "It seems possible that the Murphys knew of the major."

"It does, ma'am," he agreed. "What else can you tell me about John and Kitty Murphy?"

"Well, let me think a bit. They're from Boston—Americans, you know. He's a police officer. He's of Irish background, of course, but he says his family has been in America for many generations. I don't know what her background is. It's impossible to tell. Anyway, as I said before, three months ago they wrote to me and asked for a reservation for the first week of June."

chapter 18

After a brief moment, the inspector said, "Let's go on to your other guests, shall we? Tell me about the two young ladies from Scotland."

"Fine," Emma said, glad to be drawn away from her mounting suspicions of the Murphys. "Well, then. There's Miss Jean Blair and Mrs. Mary MacGregor—she's a widow. They're from Stranraer. I believe they're both employed at a bank there. Anyway, they were on holiday last week in Donegal. Saturday morning I received a call from the Board F'ealte asking if I could accommodate two ladies…"

"Did these women ask specifically for Sea View?" the inspector interrupted.

"I…I'm sure I don't know."

"There's a way to find out," he said, more to himself than aloud. Then, "Please continue, Mrs. Quinn."

"Yes, inspector. Well, as I said, the board called Saturday morning, and I said I could take the ladies. They arrived at tea time."

Desmond Joyce shifted a little in his chair.

"I see. Then as far as you know, the ladies are just on holiday from the bank?"

"Yes, that's right."

"Tell me this, Mrs. Quinn," Inspector Joyce shifted his great weight again in the wooden kitchen chair. Thankfully, the chair did not creak.

"How do your guests seem to be getting along?"

"With each other?" she asked.

He smiled at her honesty.

She smiled back as she answered the question. "It's a curious little group here. Morgan has taken quite a fancy to that widow. Not that anything serious has developed, I'm sure. But he does fancy her. That widow's a cool one, though. Very composed and very proper, always. Not talkative, not at all. A most attractive lady she is, though."

She was talking too fast, she knew. She tried to relax, but she was almost squirming under his gaze. She knew that he was attracted to her, and this excited her. She was trying very hard not to show it.

She continued, "Now her friend, Miss Blair, is more outgoing, really. A friendly sort. You know. Gets along well with all the other guests. Mr. Morgan gets along well with everyone too. He has fine manners. The Murphys, well, they're different."

Here her manner began to change.

"I don't know if I can discuss the Murphys without prejudicing you against them."

"Please, Mrs. Quinn. Say what you honestly think," the inspector encouraged.

Emma cleared her throat.

"John Murphy tries to act like he's everyone's best friend. He's too casual and too familiar at the same time. His wife, now, doesn't seem to like anyone or anything. She's a very unhappy woman. I suppose I should add that Mrs. Murphy had accused her husband of also being infatuated with Mary MacGregor."

"And is he?" asked Desmond Joyce.

"No, I really don't think he is. He has made a point of talking privately to her a few times. Like the other night, for instance. I guess I should tell you this."

He smiled and indicated that she should.

She couldn't help but smile in return.

"Alright. Well, I found them late the other night outside my front door. They were just talking and smoking a few cigarettes, but they seemed quite comfortable with each other. They spoke of things that weren't exactly intimate, but it was more than just casual conversation.

She stopped for a moment and then added, "I think I might have too much imagination."

Inspector Joyce said nothing, but waited for Emma to reveal more. Soon she added, "I have seen him staring at her more than once. But it's not the same kind of attention, not the same look, as when a man fancies a woman."

"What is it then?"

"Well, I don't know what to call it," was all Emma could explain. "It doesn't make sense. She's from Scotland, he's American, but they don't seem to be strangers."

The chief inspector rose from his chair.

"Mrs. Quinn, you have been extremely helpful. I won't take anymore of your time today." Then he quickly added, "I've forgotten your husband. Is he at home? I do need to talk to him."

Emma answered that he wasn't at home, that he was probably at work.

"Probably?" the inspector asked.

Emma looked away as she answered, "I assume he's at the brewery, where he works." With some embarrassment, she added, "I've no idea when he'll be home."

Quietly, Inspector Joyce said, "I see."

Before he left the room, he paused and looked at her. He lingered on her face, her hair, her slender shoulders, the fullness of her breasts.

She was aware of his scrutiny. She did nothing to stop him. She hadn't been admired in that way for many years, and she loved it.

He abruptly cleared his throat and remembered his purpose. He informed her that he would return the next morning at ten o'clock.

"I want to talk to each guest and your friend, Frances Houlihan, too."

Emma could not suppress a smile. "Oh, that'll make Francie very happy," she said.

Desmond Joyce smiled too, for he found being the recipient of Emma Quinn's smile an undeniably pleasurable experience. Then, casually, he said, "Thank you again for your help. Oh, by the way, I'm leaving a man posted here tonight."

The expression on Emma's face changed. Her smile left and was replaced by a questioning frown. Then her breath caught, a quick, barely audible gasp as the significance of his statement dawned on her.

"So you think that one of my guests is the murderer," she stated.

Inspector Joyce chose his words carefully. "I believe it would be wise of me to provide some insurance against anyone stealing out of Sea View in the middle of the night. My man will be arriving within the hour. Until tomorrow then."

He smiled. His eyes searched hers only for a moment. He tipped his hat and left.

chapter 19

Emma had just walked back to the kitchen when she heard her front door opening.

"Is 'e gone, Em?" Frances Houlihan called in.

"You know he is, or you wouldn't be here," Emma retorted. "Come on in." But Francie was already in and sat herself down on the first available chair.

"Well?" Francie demanded.

"Well, what?" Emma demanded back.

"What did 'e say?" Francie was on the edge of her seat.

"He'll talk to you tomorrow at ten o'clock."

"To me! "'E doesn't suspect me, does 'e?" Oh dear God!"

Emma groaned. "Oh Lord have mercy! The inspector will be here tomorrow at ten o'clock to talk to everyone." Her voice quavered, betraying the tension she felt.

"What's happening to my home?" she wondered aloud. "Monday was just a normal day. Things went on as usual. Yesterday it all came tumbling down around me. I don't know if I'm safe in my own home."

Before Francie could respond, Emma suddenly sat straight up in her chair. She hushed her friend with a finger placed quickly and firmly across her lips. Emma arose from her chair soundlessly. She tiptoed to the kitchen door and gingerly peeked into the hallway.

Francie assumed an offended pose. Arms akimbo, she commanded, "Would ya mind explainin' that!"

"There was someone there! Someone was listening to us. I heard them walk away!"

Francie gave her friend a disgusted look. "Oh phooey! Why would anyone want to eavesdrop on us?"

Emma sat back down. "Maybe it isn't you and me they're interested in. Maybe they wanted to know what I said to the chief inspector!"

"Well, what did ya say to 'im?"

Emma took her seat quietly. She said nothing, too confused to express her thoughts.

"Well?" Francie questioned again.

"I don't know what to think," Emma admitted. "Everyone thinks I know all about Major Fitzgerald; but really, I hardly know him—or knew him—at all. And what if one of my guests is a murderer! I might be in danger!"

Emma said nothing more.

Francie respected her need for quiet, momentarily. But she had to ask if Tommy would be home that evening.

Emma chuckled at the innocence of that question.

"How would I know, Fran?" she asked. "I never know what to expect from him. If he does come home, he'll be drunk."

Francie considered that for a minute. She seemed to have no advice to give, so she changed the subject.

"Who d'ya think was listenin" ta us?" she asked, her voice low as though she was part of a huge secret.

"I don't know that either." Emma laughed with irony. "Whoever it was ran out the front door before I could get a look at him."

"Or her!" Francie corrected.

"It's no wonder yer confused," Francie added.

But Emma couldn't tell her friend the entire story. She dare not speak of the way Desmond Joyce looked at her. She dare not tell of her body's response to this man or her thoughts of him that shocked her good Catholic sensibilities.

No, telling Francie these things would be like telling all of Howth.

Instead, she said, "I don't know who was trying to hear us."

She remembered that there would be a gard staying there tonight and said, "I guess I'll be safe enough."

chapter 20

Desmond Joyce made his way to the Howth Garda station. The spatter of rain had stopped, but he hadn't noticed. His mind was full with memories of Emma Quinn—her smile, her blue eyes, her gentle ways. Kevin Boyle and Brian Curry were waiting for him at the station and stood impressively attentive when the chief inspector entered the chambers.

"It's good that you're here, men," the chief said. "We've some planning to do."

At his request, the young men led the way to a private office. The younger receptionist followed soon after them carrying a tray of refreshments: a pot of tea, cups and saucers, ham sandwiches, cheese sandwiches and a few digestive biscuits. Desmond Joyce studied the fare, picked up a digestive biscuit and held it aloft.

"Men," he said, "Have either of you been to America?"

Amused at their puzzlement, he insisted, "Come now, gentlemen, it's an easy question!"

Garda Boyle and Curry struggled to find their voices. "No sir, no," they stammered. Both young men looked quite puzzled.

The chief inspector held the biscuit to their faces. "Take a good look at this, gentlemen. If we were in America, we'd have a glorious creation called Chocolate Chip Cookie with our lunch instead of one of these dreary things." He sighed, "Ah, well," and placed the hapless wafer back on the tray.

"I've never been there, but my cousin has, and he told me that they eat beef that's very nearly blood red," ventured Kevin Boyle, and his face turned as scarlet as the meat he dared describe. Brian Curry merely cleared his throat.

Inspector Joyce very nearly smiled.

He said, "Well then, gentlemen, let's start to work, shall we? I have some information for you, but you both must realize that what I'm about to tell you must never be repeated."

He watched their young faces and wondered if he had ever been so eager to do well and impress someone.

"Perhaps you have wondered why I am here to work on this case," he posed, and then proceeded to answer his own riddle.

"Actually, I've had a sort of surveillance here—not in person, no. There have been some undercover people from Dublin Castle here in Howth for a number of years. It's no coincidence that we've been sleuthing here since Arthur Fitzgerald reappeared on the scene. The late major has been under suspicion for a long time, even before his visits to Howth. He has been one of our prime suspects in the smuggling of money into the hands of the IRA, particularly a radical terrorist segment of it. He drives to Donegal, to various border villages. From Donegal, the money is smuggled into Ulster by someone from that branch of the IRA.

"Yes, Curry?" The inspector acknowledged the young man's puzzled look.

"Pardon, sir, but the money from where?"

"From the United States, from Canada, from Australia—from any place where Irish have emigrated. Not all the money comes from Irish people, I'm sure. There are others who hate the British enough to keep fueling our trouble. War is a profitable business."

"And with this money..."

"The radical group buys guns, finances their army!"

Boyle entered the conversation. "Getting ready for a big conflict with the British Army, is that it?"

"No, no," the inspector stated. "Probably many small attacks. You know how the IRA operated. Stab and run. Anyway, it's possible that Fitzgerald was really a double agent, carrying information back to the British.

"But sir," Boyle continued, "Why hasn't he been stopped?"

"Because he was only a messenger. We—I should say, Interpol—wanted badly to catch Fitzgerald's contacts in Ulster. It's through Ulster that the guns are purchased."

"Purchased from where?" Curry asked.

The inspector's reply was, "From the Soviet Union, the Mideast, South America. Of course there are dozens of middle men, brokers if you will, along the way."

The inspector continued, "Our man Fitzgerald and the people he worked for are very clever. Some years, the major only went to Donegal once during the two weeks he spent in Howth. Other years, he made two or three trips during his alleged holiday. And he never went to the same place in Donegal. He had various contact sites. It's also very likely he had a contact here in Howth, but we've never determined who that is. By the way, what about his auto?"

"Nothin' special, sir," answered Boyle. "The major owned a black Morris Minor 1000, of the 1960 vintage. We sent it to Dublin Castle as you requested."

The inspector helped himself to a digestive biscuit. He chewed it absent-mindedly, but after the second bite, he set it down on his plate, pronouncing "These biscuits are a waste of time."

He took a large swallow of his tea and handed his cup back to Brian Curry for a refill.

"Has there been any word back on the car?" he asked.

"Not yet, sir," Boyle answered. "What was it you were hoping to find?"

"Any sort of a clue that would lead us to his contacts. Maybe even from someone in Howth."

After a short pause, the inspector asked, "Did you send the information on those Sea View visitors to my staff at Dublin Castle?"

"That we did, sir," Curry assured him.

"You checked their passports?" The inspector took nothing for granted.

"We did, and sent that data to your staff also," Curry answered.

"No word back yet?"

"None yet," said Boyle. "But we've made it clear to our staff here that any word coming from Dublin Castle gets top priority. They must get word to either Curry or me on the spot!"

"Good men." The inspector was satisfied with the competence of these two officers. Then he asked, "Have you questioned any of the fishermen that usually saw the major after Mass?"

"We have, sir," they both assured him. Boyle continued, "They're all local pensioners. None of them knew him at all. They said that they only ever saw him talk to one man, and that on rare occasion. They don't remember anyone else talking to him."

Curry added, "They said the man might have been a local. They weren't sure. He was thin and shivering in the wind. But he had on a big coat and had his cap pulled down low on his face, so they really couldn't describe him."

"On rare occasion, you say."

"Maybe once or twice during his stay."

"They really didn't know anything more," said Boyle. Then he asked, "Do you suppose that one of Mrs. Quinn's guests could be the murderer?"

The inspector hesitated before answering. Finally he spoke. "I suspect everyone."

He stirred his tea a bit, adding a drop of milk to it. Then he said, "Boyle, I want you to spend tonight at Sea View. Keep quiet, don't announce yourself, if you can help it. Emma Quinn is expecting you. Curry and I won't be far away."

Chapter 21

The inspector reached to the food platter and helped himself to another ham sandwich. As if responding to a signal, the other men snatched up sandwiches too. Curry poured more tea, and the three men were silent for a while, each mulling over the details of their conversation while they ate. Soon the inspector stood up from his chair. He stretched his massive body and then slowly made his way to the window in the room. He stared out of it for a moment, and then without turning around, asked, "You men have lived in this town all your lives?"

Both answered affirmatively.

"Then you must know the people here very well."

"I would say so, sir," Boyle stated, and Curry agreed, "Yes, I'd say we do."

"Tell me about the Quinns," Desmond Joyce said. He turned and rejoined the others at the table. "Begin with Emma Quinn," he added without looking directly at either man.

"Oh, Mrs. Quinn," answered Curry. "She's that wonderful, she is. A very fine lady, indeed."

"She's too good for that husband of hers, and that's the truth," Kevin Boyle offered, a bit under his breath.

Desmond Joyce proceeded cautiously. "So Mrs. Quinn is not a likely murder suspect?"

Boyle answered, "Hardly, sir. She's an excellent woman."

"Why, then, did Arthur Fitzgerald stay at her home every year?" the inspector continued.

"I've wondered about that very thing," Curry responded, "And what I've come up with is that it might just be coincidence. At least it was the first year. After that, I suppose he was just that comfortable with her and she didn't bother him much. He just kept coming back."

"And she didn't ask any questions," Boyle added.

The inspector considered that possibility. "I, too, believe that occasionally the most obvious answer is the correct one," he said. Then he added, "Curry, I want you to contact the Board F'ealte. See if you can find out how the deceased made his reservations for the past eight years, if they keep records that long. And find out about those Scots women. See if they asked specifically for accommodations at Sea View."

Inspector Joyce paused a moment and then said, "Now, tell me about Mrs. Quinn's husband."

Both young men laughed.

The inspector's raised eyebrows and stern expression had an instant, sobering effect on them.

"What is the joke, gentlemen?" he demanded.

"Sorry, sir," offered Curry. "It's just that Tommy Quinn is a confirmed boozer."

"It's a well known fact that he needs to take 'the cure,' or he won't be living for long," said Boyle.

"Do you mean to tell me that the excellent Emma Quinn is married to an alcoholic?" the inspector asked of them, though he remembered the way the priest described Tommy—"*Quick, jerky movements of a drinker.*"

"That's it, sir," Boyle confirmed. "He's a fallin' down drunk."

"Does he work?"

"You might say he does," Curry responded, "But I doubt he makes it there every day."

Then Boyle proposed, "Sure and why would Mrs. Quinn work so hard at her B&B every summer if her man was bringing home full wages?"

It would have been easy for Desmond Joyce to react to this statement. He had already decided that Tommy Quinn was his enemy and not worthy of the lovely Emma. With absolute control, he asked, "Is Tommy Quinn capable of murder?"

Both garda were unsure of what to say. Boyle spoke first, "He's not been in serious trouble, but he does get feisty with a few pints in him."

Curry snickered. "Usually, he is on the bad end of a fight. He's in hospital often."

"From his drinking and his fighting," added Boyle.

Inspector Joyce was quiet for a moment. He wondered why a lovely woman like Emma would stay with a drunkard like Tommy. He asked the same of his two companions.

"Well, sir," Curry began. "She's nowhere else to go."

"No family?" the inspector asked.

"No, sir," Curry answered. "She was brought up by the Magdalenes. She left them as soon as she was old enough, and straight away married Tommy."

The chief winced at the mention of the Magdelene sisters. These Magdalene asylums were awfully punishing to girls. I wonder why she was sent there?"

"I don't know sir, but she's devout in her faith," Boyle added. "Just ask Father O'Rourke.

Desmond Joyce intended to do just that.

Curry said, "My money's on one of the guests at Sea View."

The inspector hesitated before answering. Finally he spoke. "I'm not discounting anyone." Privately, he thought, *Except Emma.*

He started to leave the room, but stopped at the door and looked back at both men and asked, "What did you find when you searched the major's room?"

Boyle answered, "We found nothing out of the ordinary. Mrs. Quinn did say that a few years ago she found some of that yellow wrapping that comes on electrical wire. The major must have brought some wire and forgot to throw away the wrapping."

This caught the inspector's attention. He wondered aloud, "Why would he need electric wire?" Then he said, "Boyle, as I said before, I want you to spend the night at Sea View. You'll stay in the room that the major used. Be very quiet. Don't announce yourself if you can help it. Keep an eye on the goings-on. Use your torch carefully and check every inch of that room."

Boyle asked, "What do I look for, sir?"

"Look for some way the major might have used that wire. Look for anything that shouldn't be there. Now get along with you. Mrs. Quinn is expecting you. Page Curry and me if anything suspicious happens."

Chapter 22

By eleven o'clock that night, June 6, 1968, Emma Quinn was utterly exhausted. Her discussion with the garda inspector had left her unnerved and shaken. She had managed to get through the rest of the day by summoning every bit of willpower she possessed. At tea time her hands trembled so, the cups and saucers clattered as she passed them around. Thank God the atmosphere during tea was subdued. Emma attempted very little conversation.

If any of the guests were aware that Chief Inspector Desmond Joyce had been there that morning, they didn't reveal it. Also, none of the guests seemed to be aware that secreted away upstairs, in the room formerly occupied by the now deceased major, was the very much alive Gard Kevin Boyle.

And hadn't he given Emma a fright! Him, dressed like a bum, knocking at her kitchen window! A disguise Gard Boyle had called it. 'Didn't want to be obvious,' that's what he said. Oh, well, she'd been able to sneak him up the stairs and into the room unnoticed, after all.

Later at supper, she had even managed to keep some food aside for the stowaway without Tommy noticing. Not that Tommy would have noticed much on a Wednesday evening. Wednesday was Tommy's card playing night, and not even the possibility of a murderer living under their roof would keep him at home.

Tommy had never had much regard for police anyway, as Emma well knew. The garda were fools, according to Tommy, and he refused to believe that one of their paying guests could be a murder suspect. Besides, Tommy always thought that the old major was a suspicious lot; if someone killed him, well, he probably had it coming.

Eleven o'clock found Emma sitting alone in her parlor. Tommy was still out at his card game. She doubted he'd make it to work in the morning. After twenty years of marriage, she had long ago stopped caring about his drinking and card playing. Be thankful for what you've got, that was her philosophy. No sense in getting upset about what you can't change. Still, tonight she would have felt more comfortable if Tommy had stayed home.

Her guests were all upstairs in their rooms. Occasionally, she heard footsteps in the second floor hallway, going from bedroom to the restroom. Every time she heard footsteps, she was frightened anew. Every time she'd had to reason with herself to keep calm. Now she was tired; tired of the tension and tired of being frightened. Nothing else to do now but turn off the telly and go upstairs to bed. But she was frightened at the very thought of doing that. Downstairs in her parlor, she felt a little removed from immediate danger. But upstairs! The murderer might be one of those people sleeping under her roof.

Emma had to steel herself to the task of going up the stairs. *Come on, girl*, she thought. *There's no boogie man. Just regular people like yourself. Desmond Joyce was just being cautious. Come on now. Kevin Boyle is there, in case there's any funny business.*

She took the steps on tiptoe, silently, cautiously, one at a time. *No sense announcing my arrival*, she thought.

She reached the top of the stairs without incident. Nevertheless, she continued on tiptoe down the hall towards her room. She passed the Murphy's door on the right, Gwillam Morgan's door on the left. Okay so far. Oh, but her heart was pounding! On down the hall, past the Scots women's door. What's that? She stopped, stood motionless.

For a minute, all she could hear was her own heartbeat pulsing in her ears.

She willed herself to calm down, to listen again.

There it was! *Plip – Plip – Plip.*

She thought herself very foolish as she realized the source of the sound. It was the bathroom sink. Someone hadn't turned the faucet off tight enough. Water was dripping from the tap.

She walked into the bathroom. *Can't let the fool thing drip all night!* she thought. She pushed the door all the way open and reached up for the light cord. She pulled the cord. Something was wrong. The light did not come on. She pulled the cord attain and again, but then her whole body was slammed against the wall! Her face, her nose burning from the impact! Her breasts throbbed with sudden pain. But her throat! Oh God! She couldn't breathe. Something tight…too tight…her throat! She couldn't…

She was lying on the floor. A face…a face above her, close to her, looking at her. Someone's hand patting her face. "There now, Mrs. Quinn. There now. Try to be calm. The doctor's on his way. Can you hear me? There now. That's right, rest."

She could see. She could see Gard Boyle's face. She could feel his hands holding hers, patting her cheek. She could not talk. She could barely breathe. Asleep again.

Now slowly, slowly, consciousness returned. She was in her bed, in her room. Other people were there. Men's voices. She could hear now. She couldn't recognize yet, but she could hear. Her eyes opened wider. Yes, definitely her room.

"She's coming around now."

A familiar voice. The doctor. Yes, she could see him.

Now another man, walking closer to the bed. Desmond Joyce.

Something had happened. Something had happened to her throat.

The doctor sat beside her on the bed. "Can you hear me, Mrs. Quinn?"

She nodded.

"There, that's fine. The inspector would like to ask you some questions. Can you talk?"

She whispered that she didn't know.

"Let me hear you," said the doctor.

"It hurts," she said, still whispering.

The doctor smiled. "I'm sure it does, dear. But I'm certain there's nothing seriously wrong. Try to answer the inspector's questions, will you?"

The doctor got up from the bed and motioned for Desmond Joyce to come closer. "She doesn't have much volume, I'm afraid. You'll have to sit close. Don't tire her if you can help it."

Desmond Joyce took the doctor's seat on the side of the bed. There was an embarrassing groan of the bedsprings, and for one crazy moment, Emma thought that if this big, big man had a wife, she pitied her.

Emma spoke first.

"You thought something would happen, didn't you?" she asked in a raspy voice.

"I thought it possible," he admitted.

"Why?"

He answered her honestly. "This morning I was sure someone was trying to overhear us. When we were in your kitchen talking, I thought I heard someone in the hall, perhaps not close enough to hear much, but worried just the same. And I'm fairly certain I saw someone peering in the kitchen window. I suspected that our spy might be threatened by you, thinking you knew more than you actually did."

As he spoke, Desmond Joyce took Emma's hand in his and began stroking her fingers.

Emma turned on her side toward him, as if this connection to him was familiar and natural. She felt safe with him there, and she was well aware of the warmth in his eyes. As she turned toward him, her bed sheet fell below her shoulder. Despite her weakness, she realized that too much of her left breast was uncovered…and she was glad. Even in her weakness, she wanted him to see her womanliness. They held hands tightly.

The doctor cleared his throat rather obviously.

Abruptly, the inspector left Emma's bedside. He glanced back to her, saying only, "You must rest now. No need to worry. Curry will be sitting directly outside your door."

chapter 23

As Desmond Joyce and the doctor left Emma's bedroom, they found Gard Boyle trying valiantly to maintain some semblance of order, for all the guests were there in the hall. Everyone was fretful, demanding to know what had happened. As the chief inspector stepped into the hall, the noise subsided. The authoritative presence of the man instantly hushed the guests.

The inspector looked from person to person. From Emma Quinn's descriptions, he could identify each one. *The blond lady, obviously, is Kitty Murphy. Rather a tacky looking female*, he thought. *The plain looking brunette in the shapeless blue robe—that's Jean Blair. The sandy-haired man must be Gwillam Morgan. The two red-haired people—funny how I mentally lumped them together—they are Mary MacGregor and John Murphy.*

Like children in the presence of a strong father figure, the guests remained quiet, not speaking until spoken to. Taking advantage of his position, Desmond Joyce chose to let the tension of the silence mount perceptibly. Then, using the element of surprise, he pounced: "How do you do, Mrs. Murphy, Miss Blair, Mr. Morgan, Mrs. MacGregor, Mr. Murphy. I am Chief Inspector Desmond Joyce."

They were completely caught off guard. They were stunned, shocked, and each looked as though he or she was guilty of something. Kitty Murphy was the first to gather her courage. She crossed her arms in front of her chest and, with a defiant toss of her head, demanded, "How do you know us already?"

Quickly, her husband hushed her.

Then Mary MacGregor, poised and cool, addressed the others.

"Chief Inspector Desmond Joyce has the reputation of seeing all and knowing all," she stated.

She smiled at him. Not a friendly smile, not a courteous smile, and certainly not an inviting smile. Actually, it was a challenging smile!

Quite a formidable female, thought Joyce, and he returned her smile for smile.

"Mrs. MacGregor is too complimentary, I'm sure," he said, rather unconvincingly. "Actually, I've observed something even now. Tell me, Mrs. MacGregor, why is it that the others here are rather sleepy looking? You alone appear to be wide awake!"

She countered, still smiling, "Perhaps the others have been asleep, sir. But I have not. I've just been reading."

With just the faintest trace of facetiousness, the inspector responded, "Have you indeed, ma'am?"

Mary MacGregor did not have to reply, for with a Quixotic flourish, Gwillam Morgan stepped in between her and the inspector. He insisted, "Now see here, inspector! I won't have you intimidating this young woman!" He put an arm protectively around her shoulders.

Desmond Joyce did not miss the surprised reaction on Mary MacGregor's face or John Murphy's puzzled expression. But with perfect aplomb, he bowed slightly, and gently let the Welshman save face.

"Of course. You are so right," he said. "At any rate, I'll be talking with each of you later this morning. Until then."

The guests returned slowly to their rooms amid much muttering and grumbling. Gwillam Morgan walked Mary to her door. Discretely, Jean Blair slipped past them and into the room she shared with Mary. Mary turned to Morgan and tilted her face sweetly up to his.

"Thank you, Gwillam," she whispered. "You were wonderful."

Morgan's face was aglow. He smiled at her adoringly. "Well, I felt I had to do something. I couldn't very well stand there and let that man put you on the spot. Besides, it doesn't pay to cower before these men. I've found that out!"

"Oh?' she questioned. "Surely you haven't been in trouble with the law?"

Morgan seemed a bit uncomfortable.

"Oh no, n-no!" he stammered. "N-not really, that is." His face flushed hotly.

Mary MacGregor continued to stare sweetly at him, which only made him more ill at ease.

"Only a minor skirmish, years ago! I was still a lad!"

Quickly, Mary MacGregor kissed him on the cheek and then slipped into her room, leaving him staring at the closed door.

Desmond Joyce and the doctor observed this little scene.

"I wonder if Morgan is telling the truth," the doctor speculated.

"I don't know," replied the inspector, "But my department is already on the way to finding out."

The doctor started down the stairs, but the inspector halted him. He asked, "Will you be here to check on Emma in the morning?"

"Certainly," Dr. Hernon assured him. Then he asked, "Will you?"

The inspector's response came in a husky voice.

"You know I will."

chapter 24

After the guests returned to their rooms, Desmond Joyce looked around the second floor of Sea View. Boyle had already locked the door to the room where Major Fitzgerald stayed. Curry was seated directly in front of Emma's bedroom door. He could see the entire hallway and the doors to each room. Curry would keep Emma safe.

The inspector would have preferred to stay inside the bedroom with Emma and keep watch over her while she slept, but he knew that would create problems. It might sully her reputation, and he didn't want to do that. But he remembered when she had turned toward him and the sheet fell away nearly revealing her left breast. He remembered clearly her unblemished ivory skin, the curves of her neck, her shoulder, her breast. He was stirred by this memory. He felt a swelling of his private part that he couldn't ignore. He wanted this woman.

He knew that he dare not indulge in this memory one second longer. He went downstairs without noticing that light was visible at the bottom of only one bedroom door, the room where the Scots women were staying.

Jean Blair and Mary MacGregor were still awake and talking quietly. Jean had been watching Mary and expressed concern for her friend, asking why Mary became so uncomfortable around the chief inspector.

"Did I seem uncomfortable around him?" Mary questioned. "I didn't feel uncomfortable."

But she was lying, and Jean knew it.

Mary sat on her bed trying to relax, breathing more slowly. She was on edge around all the garda she'd ever met. She knew why, although she could never reveal this to Jean. And she had no reason to feel guilty around garda, but she did.

"The chief inspector frightens me," Mary admitted. She hoped that Jean wouldn't ask why.

"He is a rather sizable man," Jean offered. She added, "I wonder if he suspects someone here at Sea View? I know I didn't kill the man, and I'm sure you didn't either."

They both chuckled at the thought of being suspects. Jean's laugh came easily. Mary's was brief, but she made herself keep smiling at Jean.

Then Mary changed the course of the conversation, saying, "Let's talk about something more pleasant, shall we?" She asked, "Who is caring for your cat while you're away?"

"The woman in the second floor flat is keeping her for me."

After a brief pause, she continued, "I know people think I'm a silly old spinster, always talking about my cat. But she's all I have. I'd be too lonely without her."

Mary sympathized with her. "I know what it is to be lonely," she said. "My parents are gone, and since my husband died, well… I'm fairly lonesome myself."

A Bed and Breakfast Affair

"And neither of us with a brother or sister," Jean added.

"Uh, I had a brother," Mary admitted.

"You had a brother? Did he die?"

"I don't know," Mary confessed. He ran away when he was still a boy. I don't know where he is."

"That's terrible!" Jean said. "Did you try to find him?"

"Not for many years now." She hesitated, then said, "I don't like to talk about him. It's too painful." She looked away from Jean, upset with herself for revealing that information.

Jean, ever the peacemaker, said, "Well, I count myself very lucky to have you as a friend, Mary."

Mary smiled in agreement.

Jean continued, "Do you think you'll marry again?" You're still young and attractive. Gwillam Morgan seems quite drawn to you."

"He seems like a sweet man," Mary answered. "But we live in different countries, you know. And what about you? Why haven't you ever married, Miss Blair?"

"I wanted to marry," Jean confessed. "I've only ever had one steady beau—Randy, his name was. He emigrated to Australia ten years ago. He asked me to go with him! He did!" she spoke defensively, as though she had to make Mary understand that she had once been a desirable young woman.

"Why didn't you go?" Mary asked with sympathy.

"Because...," Jean said. "That would have left my mother completely alone. She said it was okay for me to go. But I just couldn't leave her."

Jean's voice had become softer and softer as she spoke. Her voice had a wistfulness that made Mary wish she had not been so cocky.

"I'm so sorry, Jean," Mary said.

"So am I." Jean attempted a grin.

"Did you ever hear from him?" Mary asked, hopefully.

"At first—maybe for about three years after he left. Nothing in the past few years."

Then Jean stated, "Let's agree to leave the past in the past. Yours and mine."

Mary quickly agreed.

"You know, Mary, we could be in serious trouble here," Jean speculated.

"You suspect someone staying in this house, don't you?" Mary asked.

"No. I just can't be suspicious of anyone here," Jean admitted. "But I'm going to be quite cautious when we're out in the evening."

"So will I," Mary concurred.

Jean gathered her thoughts for a moment, and then she posed a question.

"I still don't understand why Desmond Joyce is investigating this. A harmless old, ex-army officer was murdered—that's all. Surely, the local garda could manage this case."

Mary responded in a half-whisper, "Maybe the major wasn't so harmless."

chapter 25

Desmond Joyce met up with the doctor at the bottom of the stairs, just as he as preparing to leave. They stopped at the front door and shook hands amiably.

"Sir, I thank you for coming to Mrs. Quinn's rescue," the inspector said. "By the way, I was never told your name."

"It's Hernon—Eamonn Hernon."

"Not a local name, is it?"

"No, inspector. I'm from the Arans, Inishmann. I came to Dublin for college and never went back home again," the doctor admitted. "I got used to the comforts here."

Before the inspector could reply, the door was pushed open, and in stumbled a very inebriated Tommy Quinn.

The man was about the same age as his wife, but his puffy red eyes, stubble of beard and gaunt appearance made him look twenty years older than he was.

"What the hell's going on?" Tommy demanded, his words a drunken slur. He slammed the door behind him and leaned back on it for support.

"Where's my wife? Emma!"

Dr. Hernon pleaded with him to be quiet. "Hush now, man. Hush. Emma's ill. I've been tending to her."

"You're lying! She's never ill! Emma!" Tommy struggled to get past them, but Desmond Joyce grabbed him and pushed him back against the door.

The inspector was thoroughly disgusted by this husband of Emma Quinn's. He wasted no words on the drunken man.

"Shut up!" he ordered in a menacing, low tone. He put an enormous fist directly in front of Tommy's nose.

"Shut up!"

Tommy Quinn cowered from the huge, angry man. He dared not say a word. The reasonable Dr. Hernon suggested they move to the parlor.

"Come on, Tom," he said gently. "Let's go and sit a bit. We'll tell you all about it."

Hernon and Joyce each took one of Tommy's arms and guided him to the parlor. Once there, they settled him on the sofa. Tommy immediately slumped to his side and curled up to sleep.

Desmond Joyce would have none of that. He pulled the man upright and gave him a good shake.

"Wake up, Tom!" he insisted, giving him some not-too-gentle slaps. But to no avail. Tommy was out cold.

Dr. Hernon pulled the inspector's hands from Tommy's shoulders.

"Never mind," he said. "He'll not hear you now."

"But I don't want him to bother Emma," Desmond Joyce stated, his voice gruff and angry.

The doctor assured him that he could take care of that.

"What will you do?"

"I'll ring the hospital and have an ambulance sent 'round for him."

The doctor picked up the telephone and made the call, asking them to come straight away but assuring them that no siren was necessary.

"Is that quite ethical?" Desmond Joyce asked. "After all, the man could just sleep it off"

The doctor shook his head. "Sadly, for the past ten years, our man here has spent most of his nights 'sleeping it off'. He's been in hospital many times. Mr. Quinn has terminal cirrhosis."

The inspector considered this for a moment. Then he asked, "Are you sure of that, sir?"

"Oh my, yes. Tommy's days are numbered."

"And if he should change his ways, stop drinking?"

"That might help some," the doctor answered. "But there isn't much chance of that. I had him in the hospital last year. I gave him the facts then, told him his liver was severely damaged. He's got a stomach ulcer, high blood pressure. I told him he had got to stop drinking."

The doctor chuckled ironically.

"You can see how well he took my advice."

A Bed and Breakfast Affair

The ambulance arrived, and the attendants quickly and efficiently bundled Tommy onto the gurney. They wheeled him out the door and loaded him into the back of the vehicle. Through it all, Tommy never stirred.

As the ambulance pulled away, Desmond Joyce turned to Dr. Hernon and said, "I guess I should fee sorry for the man, but I'm afraid all I feel is contempt."

"I know," the doctor agreed. "The real shame is Emma. She's a fine woman."

"Too good for the likes of him," the inspector declared.

"Well, you could make a case for that. Anyroad, it's a good thing for Emma that you had the presence of mind to leave an officer here tonight. Do you think she's safe now?"

"I do," the inspector stated.

"You don't expect any further attacks on her?" the doctor speculated.

"I doubt the attacker would dare to expose himself a second time tonight."

"It's a man then, our culprit?"

"Possibly. A weak man or a strong woman. Whoever it was, he or she was left handed."

Now Dr. Hernon was curious. "How do you know that?" he asked.

"It's simple," Desmond Joyce explained. "When a strangler wraps a cloth—a rope—whatever—around a victim's neck from behind, he must criss-cross the garroting agent with his hands in order for it to be effective. On most strangled victims, most of the tissue damage has occurred on the left side of the neck. Most people, including stranglers, are right handed. You see my point? On Emma Quinn's neck, most of the pressure occurred on the right side. Thus, a left-handed strangler."

He paused briefly, then began again as though thinking out loud.

"Actually, the attempt was quite clumsy. The ring around her neck is rather off-kilter, higher on the right than the left. The attacker may not have meant to kill her, only incapacitate her. I wonder…"

He became lost in his own thoughts.

"That puts a different light on it," the doctor ventured. When no response came, he stated, "Well, I'll be off now. I'll drop by in the morning to check on our girl. Can I give you a lift somewhere? Are you staying nearby?"

"I'm staying right here," the inspector answered.

The doctor was puzzled. But, by the look on Desmond Joyce's face, he knew that no more questions were welcome.

chapter 26

After he closed the door behind Dr. Hernon, Desmond Joyce went back upstairs. He found Garda Boyle and Curry standing outside Emma's closed bedroom door. He first addressed Boyle.

"Tell me what happened," he demanded.

"Yes, sir," Boyle complied. "Well, I had myself situated in the room where Major Fitzgerald had stayed. I kept the lights out in the room, and I left the door ajar. It was only open about two inches. I could just see out into the hall, you understand. No one could see me. Anyroad, it was quiet. Now and then someone would go to the loo…excuse me, sir…the restroom. But for the most part, people stayed in their rooms."

Here the inspector interrupted. "Were you able to identify the people who went into the restroom?"

"That I was, sir," Boyle assured him. "Each woman went into the loo. I couldn't see faces, but I could see robes and slippers. Funny thing is, I counted four women passing by. Now that I think about it, I saw the last woman go to the loo, but I didn't see her go back to her room. Shortly after, I heard the scuffle in the loo. When I went to investigate, I found Mrs. Quinn lying on the floor. I called for help. You know the rest."

"So you are saying that either one of the women went twice, changed her gown for the second visit and didn't return to her room, or there was a fourth woman." Desmond Joyce questioned. "What we do know," he stated, "is that four people passed your door wearing dressing gowns. We really don't know the sex of any of them, do we?"

He thought for a moment, and then asked, "Could you identify these robes?"

"Certainly, sir. The three ladies standing here in the hallway were wearing them. The American woman's was red. The Scots women each had on blue gowns, one dark and one light. Just as you saw them, sir."

"What did the fourth gown look like?"

Boyle thought about his answer before he spoke.

"It looked old. There were flowers of some kind printed all over it. Pink, they were. But it was a bit faded, as I said, not new. Oh, I nearly forgot. The woman had a big sleeping cap on. And the collar of the robe pulled up 'round her ears like she was cold or something."

Desmond Joyce's reaction to this information was instantaneous.

"Find that robe, gentlemen! Search every room in this house. Search all the luggage, even the men's. If you don't find it in the house, search outside the house. Get on it!"

The garda began their pursuit, and in spite of protests from Mrs. Quinn's guests, managed to hunt through the rooms and personal belongings. This search, however, did not turn up the elusive pink-flowered robe. The hunt continued outdoors.

Nearly an hour later, weary but triumphant, Boyle and Curry returned with the object of the search in hand.

"We've found it, sir!" Curry announced. He quickly climbed the stairs of Sea View, taking two steps at a time, to reach Inspector Joyce.

"Where was it?" the inspector demanded.

"Behind the Royal! Actually behind the dust bin in the alley."

"How odd," the inspector said. But he smiled smugly as he made the comment.

In a different tone, he continued. "Curry, you continue the vigil here for the rest of the night. Boyle, go on home. But be back here at seven a.m. Curry, at seven a.m., go to Frances Houlihan's house. Wake her and tell her to get here directly. Mrs. Quinn will need her help in the morning."

"Yes, sir," Curry agreed.

"And, Boyle, wake me when you get here at seven," Desmond Joyce said.

"Sir?" Boyle didn't understand.

"I'll be sleeping in the parlor."

"Yes, sir!"

"Oh, and Boyle—did you find any use for extra wire in the major's room?"

"Sorry, sir. I didn't get much of a chance to look."

"You and Curry get that done later this morning." With the slightest wave of his hand, he dismissed them.

chapter 27

On Thursday morning, June seventh, Emma Quinn awoke at nine a.m. For one brief moment, she couldn't imagine why her throat felt so sore and why she was still in bed. For one brief moment only, her mind was blessedly foggy. Then memory returned. Last night someone tried to strangle her. Someone had already killed Major Arthur Fitzgerald, and last night someone tried to strangle her.

She remembered Dr. Hernon and Chief Inspector Desmond Joyce there, in her bedroom, telling her she would be alright. Well, she guessed she was alright. At least she was alive.

But where was Tommy? She should have gotten up two hours ago and wakened him. He was at work now. Did he come home last night? She didn't know. If he had come home, why hadn't he come to bed? Maybe he had already gotten up and hadn't wanted to disturb her. Sure, and maybe it would snow today.

She got out of bed and paced herself slowly as she dressed, letting the haze clear from her brain. She took a good look at herself in the mirror, as if to assure herself that she was all in one piece. Her hair looked nice, the natural waves falling softly into place. But her skin was terribly pale, and the old gray housedress she intended to wear would make her look much older than her forty years.

She was late, she knew. Her guests would already be downstairs, waiting for breakfast.

Let them wait, she thought. She promptly crumpled up the gray dress, rolled it up in a ball and stuffed it in her trash bin.

She went to her closet gingerly, on wobbly legs. Last night's attempt on her life had left her weak and near to tears this morning. With great determination, she selected a newer summer dress that was a soft blue color. It made her eyes look bluer, her skin ivory instead of deathly white.

From the top drawer of her dresser, she took out her mascara and rouge and applied an ample amount of each.

There, she thought, feeling satisfied with her reflection and fortified by her make-up.

A rap on her door startled her, but she recognized the voice that accompanied it. She opened the door. There stood a very sleepy Kevin Boyle. He had watch at her door this morning.

He greeted her, asking, "Did you have a good sleep, missus?"

"I think I did," she answered, "In spite of everything."

He walked before her descending the stairs. Still, she made her way cautiously, dreading the day ahead.

It seemed as though no one was up yet, for which she was thankful.

I don't think I can manage anything at all today, she feared, and began to cry at the idea of having to cope with breakfast and her guests.

Upon opening the kitchen door, she was surprised to see her place set at the table and her friend Francie Houlihan pouring tea.

Francie set the teapot on the table with a "Hmph," crossed her arms and demanded, "Well, look at ya! "Ere I was told ya was 'alf dead, and 'ere ya are lookin' like a bloomin' fashion model!"

"I'm glad to see you too," Emma smiled, gratefully. "Why are you here so early?"

"Seems ta me I 'ad no choice," her friend stated.

Emma took a long sip of tea, trying to make sense of Francie's statement. When she couldn't fathom her meaning, Emma asked, "Just what are you talking about?"

"I thought ya'd never ask," the other woman admitted. She settled herself into a chair. "Well, din't I 'ave a summons from 'is majesty hisself, Desmond Joyce?"

"What?" Emma questioned. She was very confused.

Francie shook her head energetically. "At seven this mornin', Brian Curry come poundin' on me door. Nearly scairt me to death! Well, 'e says 'e 'as orders from the chief hisself to get me directly 'ere. "E says yer in no condition to manage this mornin' because someone nearly kilt ya last night! I dunno whether I believe 'im or not!"

"It's true," Emma assured her.

Francie looked at her skeptically. She saw Emma's freshly brushed hair, the mascara and the rouge. Then she saw her neck. She studied the still-red mark circling Emma's throat.

"Oh, me!" she said, moving closer and staring blatantly at Emma's neck.

"Is that it, then?"

"That's it."

"But why?" Francie demanded.

"Well, do you remember yesterday when you and I were talking here at the table? Remember I thought someone was listening to us from the hall?"

Her friend assured Emma emphatically that she remembered every detail.

Emma continued, "Earlier, when the inspector and I were talking, he thought someone was trying to hear us. And he thinks someone spied on us from the window."

It was Francie's turn to be puzzled.

"I'm stumped! "oose a spy, 'n why are they?"

Sadly, Emma admitted that she had no idea who was listening.

"But I think I know why," she said. "Whoever killed the major thinks I know more than I do. So the killer tried to eliminate me."

"Oh no! So the killer is one of yer guests!" Francie proclaimed.

"It certainly looks that way. Thanks be to God, Kevin Boyle was here last night. Otherwise, I might not be here this morning."

" 'Is majesty, the inspector, seems ta be very worried after yer welfare." Francie said coyly. She grinned like a Cheshire cat.

"Now why are you smiling like that?" Emma demanded.

Francie was going to enjoy this.

"Fer yer info, Missus Quinn, Desmond Joyce hisself stayed 'ere last night!"

Emma was incredulous. She said, "When I went to bed last night the only guard here was Kevin Boyle!"

"Mebbe so," Francie preened. "But after yer wee incident, the inspector spent the night right 'ere on yer divan!"

Emma was embarrassed.

"Who told y-you th-that!" she stammered.

"Brian Curry told me so," her friend said, with a self-satisfied grin.

Emma considered the information for a minute, and then asked, "Why would he do that?"

Still grinning, Francie guessed, "Mebbe 'e fancies ya."

The memory of that big man sitting beside her on her bed and holding her hands was still quite vivid to Emma. She hastily brushed the memory away, saying, "Don't be daft! Come on lady. Let's get breakfast ready!"

When Emma carried the breakfast dishes into the dining room, she discovered that Gwillam Morgan was there. His presence startled her.

"Oh, Mr. Morgan," she said with an embarrassed smile, "I didn't know anyone was down for breakfast yet."

"I didn't mean to frighten you." Morgan was obviously uncomfortable. He couldn't make eye contact with her.

He looked out the window, studied his own shoes, and examined the china...anything to avoid looking directly at Emma. But his voice was sincere. Emma didn't fear him.

"Actually," he said, "Mary and Jean and I were talking this morning. We wondered if you'd rather not have to cope with breakfast today."

She assured him that she didn't have to cope with much—that her helper would manage for her. Morgan went back upstairs to summon the others.

Francie struggled into the dining room carrying a tray heavily laden with hot pots of tea and coffee and a steaming bowl of oats. She set the tray down noisily on the table and groaned as she straightened her scrawny back.

"Oh, me poor ol' bones," she complained. "Ya've got ta get out 'o this business, Em, or else find a younger gal ta 'elp ya."

"I may be out of the Bed and Breakfast business before this season's over," Emma answered. "If Sea View gets named in the newspaper in connection with a murder, you can be sure I'll lose business."

Francie snorted indignantly. "If ya ask me, ya never should 'a let that queer ol' major keep comin' back 'ere! Very suspicious, 'e was!"

"I thought he was peculiar, but harmless," Emma defended herself.

Francie would have none of that. "If 'e was so 'armless, why was 'e murdered! An' why is Desmond Joyce hisself lookin' into the matter! "E doesn't concern hisself with just any ol' murder, ya know."

"I know."

"Knowin' that 'armless ol' man almost got ya kilt!"

Emma couldn't listen to any more. "Come on, let's make the toast," she said.

But her friend had spied a familiar car pulling up outside.

"Ya go on and make the toast," she said. "I'll go 'n open the door fer the doc."

Chapter 28

Emma went to the kitchen to prepare the toast and warm the scones, but shortly, Francie Houlihan and Dr. Hernon joined her. At this point, Kevin Boyle left the ladies, assuring them that they were in good hands.

The doctor was obviously surprised to see Emma up and about.

"You look wonderful!" he exclaimed.

He examined her neck gently. When he was finished, he said, "Well, I'm happy to report that no serious damage was done. Even so, I want you to take it easy today." Then he added, "By the way, I've just seen Tommy. He's signing himself out against my wishes. He could be on his way home now."

This information made no sense to Emma. Her face took on a puzzled expression as she said, "I don't understand what you mean."

Dr. Hernon smiled sympathetically at her. "How clumsy of me," he said. "Of course you couldn't have known." And he related the previous night's episode to her.

Emma was embarrassed and very angry with her husband. She covered her face with her hands and tried bravely to conceal her emotions. Dr. Hernon knew Emma well and allowed her some time to collect herself. Then, gently, he said, "Tommy's a sick man, Mrs. Quinn. I wanted him to stay in the hospital, both for his own sake and yours. With everything that's happened in the past few days, you certainly don't need the added worry of Tommy and his drinking. I guess what I'm trying to say is that you have to take care of yourself. The drinking is his problem and his alone."

Emma uncovered her face and smiled a little at the doctor. She agreed, "I know what you're trying to say. You know, last night I asked him to stay home with me so I would feel safer. He wouldn't, and that didn't surprise me. But for him to fall down drunk in front of Inspector Joyce, that's humiliating."

"If it's any consolation to you, Inspector Joyce thinks you are a very fine woman," Dr. Hernon assured her.

Francie jumped right in on the cue. "I knew it!" she laughed, giving Emma's hair a playful tug. "Doctor! Is Desmond Joyce married?"

"Stop that, Fran!" Emma commanded, and she stood up, frustrated and angry. She demanded that Francie go at once and check on the guests or go and do something, just get out of the kitchen. Then, regaining some composure, she implored the doctor to pay no mind to her helper.

As she was escorting him to the door, Emma saw her guests coming down the stairs for breakfast. They were all together. Even Kitty Murphy was dressed and ready for the meal.

Emma looked directly at each person, all the while holding on to Dr. Hernon's arm for security. She could feel wariness in herself as she quietly said good morning to each guest. She couldn't stop herself from wondering, *Was it him? Was it her? Which one tried to kill me?* Subconsciously, her hand touched the red mark on her throat.

There was a moment of uncomfortable silence. Then Dr. Hernon did an astonishing thing; he tipped his hat, bowed deeply, and with a booming voice as though addressing an audience of hundreds, said, "Good morning everyone! Nice to see you again!"

"Again?" Emma asked, surprised.

With a cheeky grin, the doctor explained, "We all met last night, Mrs. Quinn. These kind people were all waiting in the hallway last night when the inspector and I left your room."

"Oh, I see. I'm sure that was very nice of you all," she said, trying to prevent the irony she felt from being obvious in her voice. Then, mindful of her duty as a hostess, she added, "Come now. There's no sense in everyone standing here while breakfast is getting cold. Please, everyone, go and eat."

But Emma's mind was whirling and her legs felt weak. After eight years as a bed and breakfast proprietress, eight years of her business running smoothly, the present chaos was too much for her to comprehend. She was on the verge of tears again.

chapter 29

As the guests left for the dining room, Emma turned to Dr. Hernon.

"Thank you. That moment of moral support helped a lot. And thank you for trying to help Tommy, too."

But then, from the dining room, they heard Kitty Murphy's complaining, whiney voice.

"That so-called doctor is damned rude, if you ask me!"

And promptly came her husband's squelch, "Well, no one's asking you Kitty, so shut up!"

Dr. Hernon couldn't help but snicker. He said reassuringly to Emma, "Don't worry, young lady. Gard Curry is outside. He'll come in as soon as I tell him I'm leaving. And Desmond Joyce will be here at ten-thirty a.m. You take it easy now, and let the garda do the worrying."

"I will," she said, but not with much certainty. She was very glad to see Gard Curry coming up the walk to the house.

Emma returned to the kitchen along with Brian Curry and rested while her friend finished serving breakfast. Emma tried her best to put on a façade of calmness and strength. Inside, she felt like emotional jelly. Once breakfast was over and the guests had gone back to their rooms, Emma admitted to her friend that she was weary and near to tears. Francie poured each of them a cup of tea and sat in a chair next to Emma's.

Gard Curry posed a question to Emma. "Mrs. Quinn, could you possibly answer a few more inquiries?"

She assured him that she could cooperate.

"That's great. Do you remember telling us, Boyle and me, about finding yellow wrapping from wire in the room that the major used?"

"I do," she said.

"If you can, ma'am, try to recall just what year that was."

"I know exactly when it was," she answered. "It was the first year he stayed here. I found it when I was cleaning his room one morning."

"Did you ever ask him about it?" Curry continued.

"I did," she sighed. "I thought it might be important. I removed it from the room. After that, he asked me not to clean his room during his stay here."

"Don't worry yourself about it. Now, missus, I need to have a closer look around that room. If I could have the key, please? Thank you. I want to have the job completed before the inspector arrives."

Francie remained unusually quiet during this conversation, but when the gard left the kitchen, the woman pushed her gray strings of hair back from her forehead and adjusted her twisted glasses. Emma could tell from her friend's fidgeting that she was getting ready to say something of consequence, at least in her own opinion. Emma didn't have long to wait.

"I think I know who did it!" Francie ventured.

Emma smiled tolerantly at her friend.

"Who did just what?" she teased.

"I know who kilt the major," the Houlihan woman said slyly, tracing a scrawny fingertip around the rim of her teacup.

Emma sighed. "Well, then I guess I should ring up Inspector Joyce and tell him you've solved the case."

Francie's wiry body shook with frustration, but she feigned indifference.

"Well! If ya don't care ta know what I think, I'll just keep me ideas to meself!"

"I hope you'll share your information with Inspector Joyce." Emma teased, hiding a smile.

"I'm leavin'!" Francie declared, and she jumped up from her chair.

"Oh sit down you daft goose," Emma said, laughing aloud and glad for the relief from tension that the laughing produced. Then she reminded her friend that she was under the personal order of Desmond Joyce to stay at Sea View.

Francie plopped unceremoniously down into her chair.

"I'll make allowances fer ya, seein' as how ya 'ad a close call last night," she said

Emma reached over and took her friend's hand.

"I really do appreciate you. Please be patient with me."

Francie moved so close to Emma, their noses were nearly touching.

"And I'm tellin' ya I know who did it!" she hissed.

Emma knew it was useless to argue.

"Alright. Who?" she asked.

"Kitty Murphy!"

Emma considered this and then asked, "What proof do you have? I grant you she's disagreeable, but that doesn't mean she's guilty."

Francie sat up straighter in her chair. Summoning an authoritative posture, she stated, "I know that folks, yerself included, think I'm just a nosey old gossip. In part, that's true. But all me years o' collectin' gossip 'ave taught me more than a little bit about human nature. Now, some folks naturally 'ave a mean streak in 'em. They 'ate the whole world. They feel inferior, really. If someone else 'as somethin' they don't, well they 'ate that person. So who 'ere 'as a mean streak? Not yer shy schoolmaster from Wales. Not that plain little mouse, Jean Blair. Not yer stuck-up widow. An' certainly not yer Boston copper. Besides…"

Her thoughts trailed off for a bit. Then she jumped to alertness, this time with an entirely new thought.

"Did ya ever notice that widow and the copper starin' at each other? They could 'ardly eat their breakfast this mornin' fer starin' at each other."

For once, Emma knew her friend was right. Not about Kitty Murphy. Emma wasn't sure at all that she was capable of murder. But there was something going on between Mary

MacGregor and John Murphy. And this morning the signs were more obvious than ever before.

"You're right, Fran," she said. "I've suspected for a while now that there was something between these two."

"By somethin', do ya mean hanky-panky?" Francie suggested.

But Emma shook her head. "No, I don't think that," she said. "Though it does seem like they may be planning something."

"Well," her friend speculated, "If they're plannin' ta go off wi' each other or somethin', it surely 'appened fast. They only met four or five days ago."

Emma thought about this.

"I wonder about that. I just wonder about that."

Chapter 30

At a few minutes after ten that morning, Tommy Quinn came home. He walked in the front door of his house and went directly to the kitchen. He was surprised to find his wife and Frances Houlihan there.

"I thought you two would be upstairs cleaning rooms," he said by way of greeting them.

He poured himself a cup of tea and sat down at the table.

Emma stared at him, wondering what had happened to this man she had once loved. He had always been a bit irresponsible and ready for a pint and an argument, but he had loved her, long ago. Many things had gone wrong. Emma had wanted children, but Tommy couldn't father them. He drank more and more as the years went by. At some point in their marriage, love just died.

They still lived together under the same roof and slept in the same bed, but they hadn't made love in years. They were still married because their church demanded it...they lived in the same house because they couldn't afford to live apart. But there was no love or even affection between them.

Still, Emma felt a responsibility to him. Exhausted though she was, she asked, "Have you had breakfast?"

"Mmmm, he muttered. "Such as it was. Make me some toast, will you, Em? There's a girl."

And as she got up to do his bidding, Tommy noticed the red mark around her neck.

"The doctor said you had a close call last night," he said. Then, dismissively, he added, "Sorry I wasn't here, but all in all, you're okay, right?"

Frances Houlihan was incensed by his remark.

"Yer damn right ya shoulda been 'ere!" She shouted. "I'm gonna tell Gard Curry to come down 'ere."

Emma pleaded with her friend not to make matters worse. "What's done is done," she averred.

"Just tell 'im ta spare us any more Acts o' Contrition," Francie declared.

"You're a stupid old nuisance!" Tommy shouted at the angry woman. "And what the hell is she talking about? Brian Curry, here?"

"Both of you be quiet!" Emma demanded, and she slammed a plate on the table with a resounding crack. When she saw that both Tommy and Francie were silenced, she said, "Brian Curry is upstairs, examining the major's room. And Inspector Joyce will be here in a few minutes. He has his work to do, and he has been extremely kind to me. I would appreciate it if you do not embarrass me in front of the man." And she gave a long, steady look at her husband.

Tommy fidgeted in his seat.

"Inspector Joyce was the big man here last night with the doctor?"

"You remember him then?" Francie answered.

Tommy snorted in disgust. "How could I forget him? He threatened to punch my face!"

Francie was the first to hear the knock at the door.

"Well, speak o' the devil. I bet that's 'im now." And she was off to let him in.

When Francie left the room, Emma turned to her husband.

"Please, Tommy," she implored, "For my sake, be polite."

"Save your breath," was his reply.

In through the doorway came Chief Inspector Desmond Joyce. The huge size of the man seemed to fill the kitchen. His eyes focused on Emma Quinn, and a keen observer could have noted admiring warmth in his gaze. His voice, however, betrayed nothing. He was friendly, yet business-like. He took off his hat and nodded a greeting.

"Good morning, Mrs. Quinn. I am delighted to see you looking so well."

Then, almost as an afterthought, he noticed Tommy Quinn.

"Good morning, Mr. Quinn," he said stiffly. "I'm surprised to see you here."

"I'll bet you are," Tommy snipped.

Emma feared that an argument would start between the two men. However, Desmond Joyce was not about to waste words on Tommy Quinn. Instead, he turned his attention to Emma.

"You know my purpose here today I'm sure, ma'am," he said gently to her. "Perhaps you can suggest a room that I might use for my interviews."

Emma first offered him the use of her kitchen, as it was a hall's length away from the parlor and would afford him some privacy with the door to the dining room closed. But she realized how that would inconvenience her when he said his work could well take a couple of hours to complete.

"On second thought," she proposed, "Maybe you could use the parlor instead. Just close the doors for privacy."

"That will be fine," he assured her. "Give me a few minutes, please, and then send Gwillam Morgan to me." Then he added, "After everyone is downstairs, tell Gard Curry that I have begun my investigation. Tell him I'll send for him when I'm finished."

With that, the inspector left the kitchen.

The three people remaining in the kitchen were silent for a few seconds. Francie Houlihan spoke first posing the question, "I wonder why 'e wants Morgan first? Maybe 'e's the real suspect."

Tommy snickered at her. "Now ain't you Sherlock Holmes?" he jeered. Then he laughed out loud, "You might as well be Sherlock! That inspector couldn't tell shit from Shinola!" His laugh that followed was ugly.

Emma stood up abruptly from the table.

"Tommy, please!"

She was near to tears and bit her lower lip in an effort to keep from crying.

"Please, Tom, please."

She waited a moment and breathed deeply. She closed her eyes for just a second and then looked directly at him. Very softly, she asked, "Will you please go upstairs and tell Mr. Morgan that the inspector wants to see him. In fact, you might as well invite everyone to come down. Francie and I will make more tea."

Gwillam Morgan preceded the others coming down the steps. They were silent and awkward—Morgan perhaps more so than the others.

They had to walk down the hall into the kitchen as the inspector had already closed the parlor door from the hall. As they traipsed by to go to the dining room, Tommy halted Morgan. Menacingly, he said, "The inspector's waiting for you in the parlor."

Morgan paused briefly and then took a deep breath as he walked through the dining room to his appointment with the chief.

After Morgan had departed their company, the others situated themselves around the dining room table. People couldn't talk among themselves, the atmosphere was so oppressive. Emma and Francie brought in refreshments. Emma sent Francie to give Gard Curry the inspector's message and then joined Tommy back in the kitchen.

Jean Blair was the first to speak. She tried to seem pleasant, but her voice had a false cheerfulness in it.

"Come, everyone! Let's try to relax. Let me pour tea."

She proceeded to fill each person's cup. Still there was no conversation. Each sipped his tea and sat alone with his thoughts. Time passed silently.

Then, as if revitalized by the hot, sweet brew, Kitty Murphy livened up the situation.

"I, for one, certainly hope that we're free to leave here after today," she said.

Jean Blair welcomed the conversation.

"Oh, I hope so too, Mrs. Murphy," she said. "This has been very unpleasant."

"That's putting it mildly," Kitty Murphy stated. Then, noticing her husband and Mary MacGregor sharing a glance, Kitty Murphy added sarcastically, "Of course, maybe it hasn't been unpleasant for everyone!"

John Murphy chose to ignore his wife's insinuation, but Mary MacGregor colored angrily.

"I'm sure you're mistaken, Mrs. Murphy," she answered hotly. "No one here enjoys being suspected of murder!"

Jean Blair attempted to calm her friend. She reached over and touched her hand.

"Oh, Mary," she said, "I'm sure Mrs. Murphy didn't mean…"

"You don't have to speak for me, miss!" Kitty Murphy interrupted.

John Murphy stood up from his chair.

"That's enough, Kitty. Please, ladies. Let's all keep our heads. There's no sense getting upset."

But John Murphy's actions were not those of a calm man. He paced around the room, fists clenched, mouth set in a grimace.

Kitty Murphy preened. She watched her husband pacing, obviously worried. She asked cattily, "What's wrong, John? You seem so nervous! You aren't the murderer, are you?"

The man stopped pacing. He stood by his wife's chair, fists still clenched, his face red and angry. He spoke slowly and deliberately.

"I have had all I can take of you, Kitty."

His wife feigned a mockingly sweet smile while, embarrassed, everyone else sat in silence. Kitty looked up at her husband and cooed, "Of course you're not the murderer, dear! We all know that! It's obvious that Gwillam Morgan is the killer. That's why the inspector took him first!"

A deathly silence followed Kitty's words. Mary MacGregor stared intently at the tea in her cup. John Murphy turned his back to the women and faced the window, looking through it but perceiving nothing. Jean Blair simply sat and studied her folded hands.

For just a few minutes, Kitty Murphy let the others dwell on their own thoughts. She was enjoying the climate she had created. She picked up a scone, buttered it lavishly, took a bite and chewed it quietly, all the while smiling to herself. Then a thought occurred to her. True to her nature, she blurted it out. "You know, I'd love to be a mouse in a corner. I'd just hide in that parlor and listen to all the lies everyone tells the inspector!"

chapter 31

Had Kitty Murphy indeed been a "little mouse in a corner of the parlor," she would have seen a very anxious Gwillam Morgan enter the room. Desmond Joyce was quite aware of the Welshman's discomfort, but he chose to do nothing to allay Morgan's fears. The inspector was expert at using every advantage, and he knew that if he could keep Morgan on edge, the man would reveal far more than he might otherwise.

When Morgan entered the parlor, he immediately saw Inspector Joyce, for the very large man had seated himself in a very large armchair facing the door.

"Y-you asked to see m-me?" Morgan stammered. The inspector pointed to a straight-backed, wooden chair and directed the Welshman to sit there.

Morgan did as he was told.

"Kindly pull your chair around so we face each other," Desmond Joyce requested.

Morgan readily complied.

"That's much better, isn't it?" the inspector inquired solicitously.

Morgan quickly agreed.

Desmond Joyce shifted his great weight slowly in his chair. He was enjoying being the cat to Morgan's mouse.

"Now, Morgan," he began. Morgan squirmed a bit in his uncomfortable wooden chair. "I know a bit about you already," Joyce continued, "But there's more I need to know. I'm sure you'll be happy to cooperate with me."

"Certainly, sir!" Morgan assured him.

"Tell me then, how many times have you visited here in Howth?"

"I-I believe this is my fourth trip to Howth, sir," Morgan replied.

"And may I ask, Mr. Morgan, what is it that brings you back to Howth again and again?" Inspector Joyce seemed all courtesy and politeness, yet the steely look in his eyes left no doubt about the seriousness of this matter.

Morgan flushed and laughed nervously.

"Well, sir, for years I've been buying my clothes in Dublin. It's actually cheaper for me to take the Sea Link from Wales and buy things in Dublin than to buy in Wales. I get bed and breakfast accommodations in Howth because the B&B's are cheaper here than in Dublin proper."

Morgan laughed again.

"So you see, inspector, I use my holidays from school to travel inexpensively and to save money on new additions to my wardrobe."

"You bring your own auto with you?" Joyce asked solicitously.

"I do, sir."

"A small Fiat, black, 1964."

Morgan took a deep breath. "You've done your homework, inspector," he stated flatly.

Desmond Joyce stared silently at the very tense schoolmaster. The inspector would proceed slowly with Morgan, all the better to keep the Welshman on edge. At last he asked another question. "Why did you come to Sea View, Mr. Morgan?"

"Purely by happenstance, sir. I'd noticed this place before, and this year, just on an impulse, I decided to ask for accommodation here."

Desmond Joyce nodded his head, but did not comment on anything that Morgan said. He took his time before commencing. His next question was, "How long have you known the Murphys?"

Morgan startled. He hastily assured the inspector that he had only just met the Murphys on the day he arrived at Sea View.

"Then why did you have dinner with them on the very day you arrived here?" the inspector demanded.

"John Murphy insisted! We had no sooner met than he insisted I dine with them! Ask Mrs. Quinn if you like. She was there when we all met."

"Yes, she was," the inspector concurred, and he enjoyed the surprised look on Morgan's face. Desmond Joyce almost smiled. His next question was more benevolent.

"You are a bachelor, I believe?"

"Yes, I am," Morgan replied.

"How long have you known Mrs. MacGregor?"

"I-I only just met her, here at Sea View," Morgan stammered.

"Quite so," Desmond Joyce answered. Then he demanded, "Tell me about your previous encounter with the law!"

Gwillam Morgan sat absolutely still. His nervousness was gone, instantly replaced by ill-concealed anger.

"Why should I tell you what you already know?" he countered.

Desmond Joyce sidestepped the man's ire.

"Isn't there more to the story than what is officially recorded?"

Morgan's temper subsided a bit. He sighed deeply.

"I was just a lad, inspector. Not much past my sixteenth birthday. I got in with a crowd of older lads, bad characters the lot of them. I was with them the night they robbed that off-license, but I swear I didn't know the one lad had a gun. When he shot that shopkeeper, I was so frightened that I cried. Anyway, the judge believed me. I was given probation. I never had to do any time in prison."

Inspector Joyce waited in silence, as though considering Morgan's statement. Morgan grew uneasy, and after a few minutes, requested to know if anything further would be asked of him.

The inspector replied slowly, "There is just one more question. Whom do you think murdered Major Arthur Fitzgerald?"

Morgan was appalled.

"I'm sure I couldn't point a finger at anyone in this house, sir! I don't know who killed the major, but I think you should look elsewhere for your killer!"

Desmond Joyce acknowledged Morgan's opinion.

"Thank you, Mr. Morgan. I don't think I need to ask anything else of you. Oh, just one thing, please. Do you have the time, Mr. Morgan? My watch does not seem to be working."

Morgan looked quickly at the watch on his left wrist.

"It's eleven a.m.," he replied.

"Fine, fine. Thank you, sir. Please ask Miss Jean Blair to come in next. Oh, and Morgan, are all the guests in the dining room? Good. Tell them they should remain there for the time being."

chapter 32

In a few minutes the door to the parlor opened again, and a timid Jean Blair entered the room. Desmond Joyce studied the young woman's appearance. *What a nondescript woman*, he thought. *Hair not blond, not brown. Eyes not green, not brown, not even hazel. Boxy looking suit—maybe a gray shade, not really blue. No makeup. Certainly no sex appeal.*

Jean Blair cleared her throat slightly. Rather hesitantly she inquired, "You asked to see me?"

"I did indeed," Desmond Joyce answered, far more gently than he had spoken to Gwillam Morgan. "Please sit down, Miss Blair," he said, and he motioned toward the wooden, straight-backed chair.

Jean Blair promptly sat in the offered chair and primly adjusted her skirt so that her knees were covered. Her sensibly shod feet were set very correctly together.

"I believe that you are employed by the Bank of Scotland at Stranraer, is that not correct, Miss Blair?" Inspector Joyce asked.

When she confirmed his statement, Desmond Joyce continued, "How long have you been employed there?"

"Nearly twelve years," she answered quickly, but with a quavering voice.

"Why don't you just tell me about yourself," the inspector invited. He shifted a bit in his chair and gave a small wave of his hand, signaling her to begin.

"Well," she began, "There isn't much to tell. I live alone. My mother and I shared a flat until she died last year. She left me a bit of money—not much, mind you. Just enough that I can stay in my flat and take a holiday now and then. That's about it. I live quietly. Just my cat and me."

"Fine. I believe Mrs. MacGregor is also employed at the Stranraer bank?"

"She is, sir."

Desmond Joyce leaned back in his chair and assumed a more relaxed attitude. He implored Jean Blair to try to relax also. Indeed, the poor young woman seemed ready to weep.

"I'm sorry, inspector," she apologized as she dabbed at her eyes. "It's just that I've never been involved in any sort of trouble before. It's really very unnerving."

Desmond Joyce waited while the young Scots woman regained her composure. Then he said, "Please don't upset yourself unnecessarily, Miss Blair. Just answer my questions as truthfully as you can, and this interview will be over directly."

She smiled bravely, and the inspector took this as a sign to continue his interrogation.

"How long have you known Mrs. MacGregor?" he asked.

She thought for just a moment and then said, "I think it has been about three years. I met her when she came to work at the bank."

"I see. And did you know her husband?"

She assured him that she had never known the late Mr. MacGregor.

"Mary was very recently widowed when I met her," Jean explained.

Desmond nodded his head in comprehension.

"And the two of you take your holidays together?" he asked.

"This is the first holiday we've taken together," she answered.

"You decided to travel in Ireland?"

"Yes. Neither of us has been here before."

Desmond Joyce paused to formulate his next question.

"I want you to think carefully about the answer to this next question—whose idea was it to visit Howth?"

Jean Blair was obviously puzzled. She stammered, trying to answer.

"I-I-I don't know. We, we both wanted to see the Dublin area, and we both agreed to look for bed and breakfast accommodations in Howth."

"I see. And how did you happen to come to Sea View specifically? It was Mrs. MacGregor who called for the reservation," Desmond Joyce surmised.

"Yes, sir," she agreed.

Then, as there seemed to be no more questions to answer, Jean Blair asked if she was free to leave.

Desmond Joyce rose from his chair. Actually, he extricated himself from it, albeit adroitly.

"Certainly you are free to leave, Miss Blair. If first, you will kindly tell me the time."

Jean Blair gave a surprised little laugh. She pulled back her left sleeve and informed him that it was now eleven-twenty a.m.

Desmond Joyce bowed courteously to the young woman and escorted her to the door.

"Thank you, Miss Blair," he said. "And if you please, ask Mrs. MacGregor to come in next."

Chapter 33

Desmond Joyce walked to the parlor window. He stood there for a few minutes, looking at and admiring Emma Quinn's flower garden. *So lovely, yet so unassuming*, he thought.

He had to admit to himself that these adjectives applied equally to the garden and to Mrs. Quinn. *If I were ever to marry*, he thought, *I would choose a woman like Emma Quinn.*

His thoughts were interrupted by a strong, defensive female voice.

"I believe you summoned me," Mary MacGregor stated.

Desmond Joyce turned slowly, deliberately, and faced the young widow. Mary MacGregor was standing at the door. Her posture was stiffly erect. She looked *en garde*, ready to strike.

The inspector immediately chose to keep her vexed.

"How kind of you to see me," he said with a hint of sarcasm in his voice. It was effective. Mary MacGregor's eyes narrowed. The muscles in her jaw locked for a moment—just a moment. Then she regained control.

"May I sit down?" she asked with mock courtesy.

"By all means. Forgive my lack of manners," he countered facetiously. He allowed her only enough time to get to the chair when he demanded, "Mrs. MacGregor, tell me why you asked for accommodations here at Sea View."

She shrugged her shoulders innocently. "But I didn't," she stated. "I simply asked the Board to find us twin accommodations in Howth, and they directed us to Sea View."

Inspector Joyce smiled knowingly.

"Very curious," he said. "The Board's records show that you asked specifically for Sea View."

MacGregor's cheeks colored hotly. She emphatically contradicted him, saying that she had asked for a room with a sea view, not Mrs. Quinn's house.

The inspector chose not to argue the point. He walked to his chair, positioned his great body well back into it, crossed his legs and simply looked at her. His only utterance was, "Hmmm." Almost as an aside, he requested, "Tell me about yourself."

"What would you like to know?" she questioned, not at all comfortable.

"Tell me about your late husband."

With obvious sarcasm, she responded, "Why on earth would he interest you?"

Desmond Joyce fixed a riveting look upon her.

"He doesn't interest me at all, but you certainly do. I find you a compelling person."

"I handle my grief in my own way," she said, "And I don't like to talk about him. I'll tell you that he died of Leukemia. That's all you need to know. Besides, you can find out anything. I know you have connections in Scotland."

"Very well," the inspector conceded. But he countered with, "Then tell me what you know about the late Major Arthur Fitzgerald."

"The only thing I know about him is that he is dead."

"Indeed?" the inspector countered.

"Indeed!" she stated.

"You hadn't heard his name before coming to Sea View?" he asked.

"Indeed I had not." Mary MacGregor was the essence of politeness.

"And I suppose you are a born and bred Scots woman," Desmond Joyce smiled.

"I am," she smiled back.

"Never been to Ireland before?" he dared, courteously.

"Never," she said sweetly.

"Why don't I believe you?" he grinned.

She got up and left the room.

Chapter 34

A few minutes later, Kitty Murphy knocked boldly at the parlor door. She didn't wait to be invited in; she pushed the door wide open and closed it absentmindedly. Indeed, she was too busy talking.

"John and I flipped a coin, and I lost, so I'm next," she announced. And she came in and audaciously situated herself in the wooden chair.

"Well," she demanded, "Ask away. I've got nothing to hide. But what did you say to that redhead? She's boiling mad!"

Desmond Joyce truly had to laugh at this brassy female.

"I am sure you have nothing to hide, Mrs. Murphy," he assured her. "And I have very little to ask you."

"Ask anything you like," she offered with a magnanimous sweep of her right hand.

"If you insist," the inspector agreed. "Let me begin by asking you why you wear your watch on your right wrist?"

Kitty Murphy looked at Desmond Joyce as if he were crazy.

"Because I'm left-handed," she answered incredulously. "All left-handed people wear their watches on their right wrists. John is left-handed too. And you know what? That red-headed widow is left-handed too. And Gwillam Morgan is ambidextrous. He can…what did you say?"

"Oh, I was just thinking about muddied waters," he sighed.

"Well! I would think you'd try to pay some attention to my testimony!" she scolded.

"How lax of me." He struck his chest. "Mea culpa."

"What's that? she asked.

"Nothing worth repeating. Let me change the direction of this conversation, if I may. Tell me about the other evening when you and your husband dined at the Abbey Tavern."

"Well it sure wasn't worth what it cost us to eat there," she complained. "It was so crowded…"

"Excuse me please," Desmond Joyce interrupted. "Let me be more specific with my questions. What time did you arrive at the restaurant?"

"At seven, but we had to wait…"

"Yes, yes," he interjected. "And you stayed for the ballad singing?"

Kitty must have realized that she might as well be concise. She said, "Yes."

"The ballad singing lasts from nine p.m. to eleven p.m., I believe?"

Tersely, she said, "Yes."

"You left the restaurant at eleven and went where?"

Kitty guffawed! "We came right back here! Where else can you go in this country at eleven p.m.? They roll up the sidewalks here."

"Please, Mrs. Murphy!" the inspector demanded. "Keep to the subject, I beg you."

"I'll do my best," she replied dryly.

Desmond Joyce had grown weary of this tiresome, complaining woman.

"I have just a few more questions for you," he said, more to reassure himself than her. "Let us be as direct as possible."

"Whatever you say," Kitty said, innocently.

Desmond Joyce silently prayed for patience.

"Tell me, if you will, were you and your husband ever separated during the evening?"

"Absolutely not," she stated.

He considered this for a moment. Then he asked, "Neither one of you left, even perhaps to make a trip to the restroom?"

"Oh, John did, once. He was gone a while, too."

"At what time was this?"

With a shrug of her shoulders, Kitty Murphy stated that she wasn't in the habit of timing her husband's bathroom visits.

"Oh, come now, Mrs. Murphy! I'm sure you keep very close watch on your husband!" Desmond Joyce leaned forward and pinned Kitty with a menacing stare.

"I repeat! What time did your husband leave your table?"

Meekly, she admitted, "It was nine forty-five p.m."

"And what time did he return?" Desmond Joyce roared.

"About fifteen or twenty minutes past ten p.m."

"Thank you! Good day, Mrs. Murphy!"

Chapter 35

While he was waiting for John Murphy, Desmond Joyce was considering how he would interrogate this man. In all his years with the Garda, the inspector had never had to question another law enforcement officer as a suspect in a murder. He hadn't long to plan his position, however, for not more than two minutes had elapsed between Kitty Murphy's exodus and John Murphy's arrival.

The American policeman seemed tentative as he entered the room. The first words he said, in fact, were an apology—for his wife.

"I hope Kitty was cooperative. Lately she's been really hard to get along with. This trip was my idea. She didn't want this."

Desmond Joyce said nothing. He decided to let John Murphy interrogate himself.

"Actually, Kitty isn't usually miserable. When I started talking about coming to Ireland, she changed. She's been really nasty since the day we got here."

He paused for a moment.

"I think it's these B&Bs that she doesn't like, really. I mean, she doesn't like having to live so intimately with other people. And then when she saw all the extra attention that poor old Major Fitzgerald was getting, well, she was… well, no sense getting into that right now, is there?"

John Murphy gave a self-conscious laugh.

"I guess I'm talking too much. You're in charge here."

The inspector accepted John Murphy's apology with a quiet wave of his hand. He asked simply, "Is it your first trip to Ireland?"

"It sure is. I've been wanting to make this trip for years, though. My grandparents were from Ireland. I've always wanted to see their home."

"And where is their home?"

"Dublin. Although I don't know exactly where in Dublin."

The American leaned back into his chair and crossed his legs. Now he seemed perfectly at ease. He went on.

"It's really a shame that this had to happen. The murder, I mean. It kind of spoils the vacation, if you know what I mean. Do you have any idea how long we'll be detained here? I mean, what motive could any of us have for killing the major? Hell, none of us even knew he existed."

One eyebrow raised. That was all Desmond Joyce had to do. John Murphy stopped talking instantly.

"You came to Sea View upon the recommendation of your friends, the Burkes, I believe."

"Yes, we did," Murphy answered cautiously.

"And the Burkes never mentioned the name of Major Arthur Fitzgerald?" the inspector challenged.

"Never!" John Murphy's temper rose.

"Isn't that curious?" was the inspector's only comment. He waited, obviously studying the American. Desmond Joyce's impassive face gave no clue as to what he may or may not have been thinking. His next question came as something of a surprise to Murphy.

"Did you enjoy your evening at the Abbey Tavern?" The inspector smiled kindly.

John Murphy was obviously relieved at this change in the line of questioning. He exhaled deeply and ran his hand across his slightly sweaty brow.

"Sure I did," he said. "The food was great, the service was great, and the ballad singing was swell."

Desmond Joyce moved right in. "It's a shame you had to miss some of the ballad singing. Your wife told me you excused yourself to go to the loo, and you were gone for half an hour."

"I was no such thing! I went to the loo, but I was gone only ten or fifteen minutes! When I got back, she was so busy complaining to a couple at the next table, she didn't even notice me."

John Murphy took a couple breaths and then continued, "Inspector, I'm sure you've guessed by now that my wife is a trouble-maker. She'll say anything—anything at all, just to keep things stirred up. I don't suppose she mentioned that she left the table at the same time I did—for the same purpose. She must have gotten back to the table a couple minutes before I did."

"Now that's another curious thing," Desmond Joyce remarked. "You know how women always complain about their loos—long line waiting to get in. That night must have been no exception. Or perhaps you didn't return to your seat straight away."

"Well, I did look around for Jean and Mary."

"Did you find them?"

"I did," Murphy answered guardedly. "I waved to them, but they didn't see me. They seemed really into the music."

The inspector smiled a conspirator's smile.

"Your wife left out some details, apparently." Then he added, "What is your wife's ethnic background?"

Murphy was again surprised by the change in the interrogator's direction.

"Kitty? She's Irish, too. She was born in Ireland but raised by an aunt and uncle who had emigrated to America."

"Indeed?" Desmond Joyce digested this bit of information. "Why was she raised by an aunt and uncle?"

"Her parents gave her to them when she was just a baby. She was the tenth child in the family. They weren't well off, didn't have much."

With a trace of irony in his voice, the inspector surmised, "That could explain a lot."

Then, leaning a bit forward in his chair, Desmond Joyce said, "Just one more question, if you don't mind. How long have you known Mary MacGregor?"

John Murphy couldn't disguise the alarm that tensed every muscle in his body. He breathed in deeply and didn't exhale immediately. He was cautious. In quiet, measured tones, he finally responded by saying, "I met her the day we arrived at Sea View."

The inspector did not comment on his answer. He simply uttered, "You may go now."

Murphy left the room.

Chapter 36

Desmond Joyce wasn't alone long. Frances Houlihan must have been waiting her opportunity, for no sooner had John Murphy left the room than she came bursting through the door.

"I guess I'm next," she announced happily and sat herself down in the chair opposite the inspector. "Where d'ya want me ta start?" she offered eagerly.

After the strain of the past hour's questioning, the inspector was almost glad to talk with the obviously simple woman. He felt generous and decided that he would flatter her ego.

"Tell me," he asked with an obvious air of the confidant, "Who do you think killed the major?"

Francie slid herself close to the edge of her chair and thus much closer to Desmond Joyce. She looked quickly to her left and her right as though an eavesdropper might be hiding in the room. Then, in a hushed voice, said, "I'll tell ya wha' I think. I think Kitty Murphy did it."

"I see." The inspector gave this statement his full consideration. He was enjoying this. He knew his next question would boggle her mind, but he asked, "And did she have an accomplice?"

"What!" Francie gasped. "Ya think I'm right! An' someone helped 'er?"

Desmond Joyce chuckled. He said warmly, "At this point, Mrs. Houlihan, I'm not discounting the possibility of anyone being guilty."

Francie didn't like being the object of his chuckles. Indignantly, she crossed her skinny legs, then crossed her puny arms and stated, "Hmmph! If ya din't want me opinion, ya shouldn't ask fer it!"

Desmond Joyce arose from his chair. He walked to the door, opened it, smiled at her and then indicated that she was free to leave.

It took a minute for her to realize what was transpiring. When she did understand, she huffed up from her chair and stomped off. But as she was leaving the room, the inspector gently called her back.

"Please, Mrs. Houlihan," he said quietly, "I'm not free to discuss my suspicions at present. Let's just say that I think I'm on the right track. And I must ask you to keep that strictly confidential."

Francie fairly swelled with importance. She glanced around quickly—making sure no one was within earshot. Then she whispered, "Ya can count on me, inspector!" And she tiptoed away.

When he was sure that Francie was too far away to see him, Desmond Joyce left the parlor and went upstairs to find Brian Curry. He opened the door to the room formerly occupied by Arthur Fitzgerald. There was the garda officer, on his hands and knees, examining the woodwork with a powerful torch.

"Any luck?" Inspector Joyce asked.

"Quite a bit, sir," answered the affable Curry. "See for yourself."

He moved to the closet and crawled inside. Desmond Joyce wasn't about to crawl in after him. Instead, he got as close as he could and bent down as well as he could, and he saw what Curry's torch was shining on.

There in a corner was a hole in the plaster. It was on the outside wall of the closet and so small it could easily be missed. The closet had no light of its own, and without a strong torch, a person would never see the hole for it had a new smear of plaster over it. Curry had scraped away the fresh plaster and found the hole that went all the way through to the outside of the house.

"What do you make of this?" Curry asked.

"A hole is made so something can be passed through it. No doubt, whatever passed through here was connected to the wire that the major so conveniently left us clues to."

Desmond Joyce considered the puzzle for a moment, but it was Brian Curry who guessed the correct answer.

"I've got it! He exclaimed. "The major had to have some way to communicate with his partners in crime. He certainly couldn't use Mrs. Quinn's phone. Maybe he had a short wave radio or a Morse code—whatever that machine is called. Anyroad, he had something that required an antenna. This hole is just about the right size for a radio antenna to pass through."

"You're a genius," said the inspector. "We've tried for years to find out how Fitzgerald communicated with his conspirators. This is the best theory so far."

chapter 37

Francie Houlihan returned to the kitchen, very pleased with herself. She hummed a little tune while she fairly sauntered around the room. Finally, she paused by the chairs where Emma and Tommy Quinn were seated, and posing impressively, asked, "Well, don't ya want ta know what 'e asked me?"

Tommy Quinn snorted derisively. "I can just imagine what a help you were to that man," he jeered.

"Ya hush yer gob or so help me God, I'll..." and Francie drew back a fist, ready to punch Tommy squarely in the mouth.

Tommy moaned in mock fright and waved his arms frantically before his face, pretending to be terrified of Francie.

"Oh, don't hit me, don't hit me!" he teased.

"Stop it you two!" Emma demanded, trying to restore some order in the kitchen. At any other time, she probably would have ignored the altercation between her husband and her friend; today, however, she was very much aware that Desmond Joyce, Chief Inspector of the Garda Siochanna, was present in her home.

A Bed and Breakfast Affair

She was also honest enough to admit to herself her awareness of Desmond Joyce as a man. She remembered very clearly him sitting on the edge of her bed, comforting her, holding her hand the night someone had tried to strangle her, the night her husband wouldn't stay home with her.

She knew that Desmond Joyce cared for her. She was flattered by his obvious attention. She also felt very guilty about the whole matter. *And how will I confess this to Father O'Rourke?* she thought.

When she allowed herself time to reflect upon the events of the past few days, she was amazed at the things that had happened to her. For the past twenty years, Emma Quinn had been a typical Irish housewife—no, not typical, for she had not been blessed with children. But her life had been acceptable. Her marriage had been less than perfect. In fact, it had been a disappointment. But what was to be done about it? Absolutely nothing. In the eyes of her church, and thus in her own eyes, she and Tommy would be man and wife until death parted them. Since Tommy had not been the husband she had hoped he would be, she had looked for companionship and fulfillment elsewhere. And she found it in her church, her friends and her summer work as a bed and breakfast proprietress.

And now, even these comforts had been turned against her, it seemed. One of her guests had been murdered, her own life nearly ended, and it seemed that the perpetrator of these crimes was someone staying under her own roof. She really thought that this would be her last summer in the bed and breakfast business.

There was another man in her life now—so far, quite innocently, but this man could be someone she could care for. This would be offensive to her church. No, nothing good could come of this. *And nothing good can come of this daydreaming either*, she reprimanded herself. She rose from her chair and literally shook herself back into reality.

"Quiet, you two. Quiet! Everyone in the house can hear you!" she demanded of the still bickering foes.

Francie and Tommy had evidently run out of epithets, for they quieted themselves without further demands from Emma.

"Now then," Emma said, more satisfied with the atmosphere in her kitchen, "Fran, please sit down and tell us what you can about your talk with Desmond Joyce."

Nothing could have pleased Fran more.

"Funny ya should put it that way, 'tell us what ya can', ya said, 'cause that's exactly what the inspector cautioned me about. Keep it all under yer 'at, 'e says ta me. So, as I promised 'im I'd do jest that, there's nothin' I can tell ya. Wild 'orses couldn't drag it out o' me!" And she waved her right arm through the air as if sweeping temptation out of her way.

Tommy Quinn fairly exploded with laughter, "Oh my God," he said wiping tears from his eyes. "My God, that's a good one. My bet is that you didn't know anything to tell, and Desmond Joyce didn't know the difference!" And Tommy guffawed and roared.

The more he laughed, the more Emma hated him. She wondered what cruel twist of fate had put him in her life. She pounded the table in front of him and screamed, "Shut up! Shut your horrible mouth!"

Tommy met her gaze, but only for a moment. Abruptly, he went into the pantry. On the pantry floor, in the kitchen coal bin, he dug down to the bottom of the coal and found what he had hidden there—a pint of whiskey. He wiped his soot-covered hands on his trousers and wiped the top of the bottle with Emma's dish towel. Then he poured a generous dollop of whiskey into his teacup. He took a long swallow of the amber-brown liquid and wiped his mouth with the back of his hand. He looked directly at his wife.

"No YOU shut up," he said. And at that moment, Desmond Joyce walked in through the kitchen door.

"Right on cue, inspector!" Tommy Quinn greeted and raised his cup in a mock toast.

Desmond Joyce said nothing. Indeed, he dared not allow himself to respond to Tommy Quinn. To control his anger, he also had to control his speech. But his thoughts would have startled everyone in the room, for he was thinking, *Go on you miserable sot! Drink up and kill yourself off with it! The sooner, the better!*

Emma Quinn was thoroughly embarrassed. Her humiliation was ill-concealed as she rose and approached the chief inspector.

"I'm so very sorry," she began, but he would not allow her to say more.

"You have nothing to apologize for, Emma."

But as soon as he had addressed her by her given name, he knew he had made a mistake. Tommy Quinn heard this use of his wife's familiar name, and he was quick to react to it.

"Oh, so it's 'Emma' now, is it?" he taunted. He raised his cup of whiskey and took a long, deep drink from it. He rose from the table, and picking up his bottle, announced that he was leaving.

"Me and my friend, 'Old Bushmills,' here," indicating his bottle, "We will find some more congenial place to spend some time."

He tripped on the door step on his way out.

After his departure, nothing was said for a few seconds. Then, very gently, Desmond Joyce asked both Emma and Fran if they would talk with him for a few minutes longer. His eyes never left Emma's face as he said those words.

Francie saw the looks that he and Emma exchanged. She said, "I thank ya fer the invite, sir. But ya don't need me here."

She prepared to leave, but he stopped her, asking her to stay.

Apologetically, he said, "Emma, I must leave, and I don't want you to be alone. If Mrs. Houlihan will stay with you, it will ease my mind a bit." He smiled tenderly at Emma, and she at him.

Turning to Frances Houlihan, he stated, "As chief inspector for the County Dublin, I'm directing you to remain at this house for the next twenty-four hours."

"Ya mean I hafta sleep 'ere?" Francie questioned.

He assured her that she did. Then he added that Garda Boyle and Curry would be staying also.

He touched Emma's hand and assured her he would return the next day.

chapter 38

Thursday evening, June seventh, found Emma, Francie and Garda Boyle and Curry all together at Sea View. Emma was extraordinarily tired. The events of the previous night had taken more of a toll on her mind and body than she had ever experienced before. But she dreaded going to bed.

Conversation among the four persons was easy, focusing on local people and happenings. However, Emma kept remembering Dr. Hernon being there. And she especially remembered Desmond Joyce sitting on her bed holding her hand, and him smiling at her this morning with the kind of warmth in his eyes that every woman recognizes. Just thinking about the man stirred her, made her heart beat faster. Her memories were abruptly interrupted by Gard Boyle.

"Mrs. Quinn?"

"Oh?" she startled. "I'm sorry. Did you ask me something?"

Boyle smiled kindly at her. "I just asked, do you know where your husband is tonight?" He asked the question as gently as possible.

"I-I'm sure I don't," she stammered. With a tiny bit of guilt, she realized that she didn't care where Tommy was or what he was doing.

"I'm sorry, Kevin," she said, "But I have no idea where he is. He left here this morning with a pint of whiskey in his hand. But a pint wouldn't last him very long. You might check at his pub. Maybe he's there."

She gave the idea another moment's consideration and added, "Maybe he's back in hospital. Call and ask."

"Yer better off without 'im," advised Francie. "Besides, I think a certain important inspector is…"

She was cut off in mid-sentence by Emma's curt demand that she stop talking immediately. "Your imagination is working overtime," Emma accused.

Francie chuckled. "I know all the signs, ya know, of when a man fancies a woman."

Curry and Boyle snickered at this statement. Boyle ventured, "You've been fancied more than a few times, Fran. Right?"

Francie preened like a regal cat, pretending modesty.

Brian Curry, however, suspected the real meaning of her statement.

"What are you saying?" he asked her. "Does Inspector Joyce fancy Mrs. Quinn?"

"I think all the signs are there," she stated.

Curry turned quickly to his partner. "Boyle, remember the other day at the station? Joyce was asking us all those questions."

But Boyle wouldn't allow this to go on. "Boy-o," he said, "You'd better stop right there."

"You're right, of course," said a chastened Brian Curry.

Francie wasn't ready to let go of the conversation.

"Oh, don't stop now!" she demanded. "Ya gotta tell me what 'e was askin' about! Was 'e askin' about Em?"

"No, no Fran. We shouldn't talk about it," insisted Curry.

"Just tell me this," she persisted, "Is the chief inspector married?"

Emma Quinn groaned. She turned away from the others in a vain attempt to hide her embarrassment. Angrily, she declared, "It doesn't matter if he's married or not! I AM!"

She took a few deep breaths. No one said a word. Then she apologized saying, "I'm sorry. I'm not myself tonight."

She didn't realize how much she had revealed with her previous statement.

A short but strained pause followed. No one knew what to say, and no one wanted to be the first to speak. With an air of resignation, Emma stood up from her chair and asked Francie if she was ready to go upstairs to bed.

"I'm really tired," she admitted. "I hope you don't mind if we go up early."

"Go on, girl," her friend answered. "I'll be right along."

Emma had no sooner left the kitchen than Francie took Brian Curry by the arm and pulled him closer.

"Is 'e married?" she repeated, more in a hiss than a whisper.

Curry made eye contact with Boyle, as if asking his permission to answer the question. A grin from Boyle was all the license he needed. He whispered back to her, "No, he's not married. He never has been."

She was delighted.

Half an hour later, the two women were settled into the double bed that Emma usually shared with Tommy.

"I don't think Tommy will be coming home tonight. He may never come home again," Emma said aloud, but as much to herself as to her friend. For once, Francie made no reply.

A moment later, Emma spoke again. "When did things start to go wrong between Tommy and me?" she asked.

"'ow should I know?" Francie grumbled. She would have welcomed the chance to go to sleep.

"I wasn't asking you. I was only thinking out loud."

"Well, think out loud a bit quieter."

In reply, Emma gave Francie a friendly nudge in her back with an elbow. Then she asked, "I wonder where Boyle and Curry will station themselves tonight."

Francie turned over to face her friend.

"Brian Curry will be sittin' on a chair right outside yer door 'ere. And Boyle will be sittin' downstairs in the parlor where 'e can see the front door, jest in case yer better 'alf does come 'ome."

She hesitated a second.

"Don't ya wanna know where the chief inspector is? "'e's next door at the Royal." Francie giggled.

Very quietly, Emma asked, "Do you really think he fancies me?"

"I know 'e does." She was certain. With the air of a conspirator, she asked Emma, "Do ya fancy 'im?"

"I dare not let myself. Now go to sleep."

But Francie wasn't finished teasing her friend.

"Think ya might dream about 'im?" she chortled.

"Stop it!" Emma insisted. "Besides, I haven't been in love in so long…"

Now her friend was laughing.

"Don't worry about that part," she said. "I think it's like ridin' a bicycle—ya never forget 'ow!"

Francie fell asleep quickly. However, for Emma, sleep was elusive. Her mind would not allow rest to come. Old memories paraded through her consciousness like noisy foot soldiers.

Her life had spun out of control. It seemed to her that she was nothing but a puppet being pulled here and there by unseen forces. But she really didn't want to return to life as usual because now she was in love. She had to let herself think the word, love. All the chaos had brought Desmond Joyce to her, and being with him made her feel wonderful.

Downstairs, Kevin Boyle and Brian Curry were deep in discussion about the recent excitement in Howth, for the murder of Arthur Fitzgerald was the topic of everyone's gossip. The term, "sleepy little village' could have originated in Howth. Nothing ever happened in Howth.

Boyle and Curry were the only garda in Howth. There was a superior officer, of course. But he was just a couple months away from being pensioned, and he preferred to spend his time fishing. Even so, Captain Festus Malloy had heard the gossip and found it necessary to show up at the garda station earlier in the day.

While Curry was crawling about at Sea View, Boyle was bearing the brunt of Captain Malloy's ire. He wanted to know why he hadn't been notified immediately when the murder was discovered.

"Thanks be to God, Desmond Joyce came into the station," Boyle told Curry. "He was that smooth with Malloy. He made the sarge feel like he was relieved to see him."

"That's how he got to be chief inspector," Curry surmised. "He knows just how to handle people."

Boyle snickered. "Going by what Francie said, the inspector wants to handle Emma Quinn!"

Curry grinned. "Yeah. Too bad Tommy Quinn is in the way."

chapter 39

It was mid-morning the next day, Friday, June eighth, that Desmond Joyce returned to St. Michael Church. As he approached the church, he could see the elderly Father O'Rourke working in the garden. The priest was carefully pruning rose bushes and while doing this, seemed to be rocking and swaying his body in time to some silent melody.

This was indeed an odd sight; a small, frail old man whose black cassock hung far too loosely from his rounded, thin shoulders, his occasional shocks of white hair so sparse that the sun shone through them. And he, bending, dipping and sidestepping, trimming bushes in time to some rhythm only he could hear.

Desmond Joyce approached the garden as quietly as possible in order to continue observing the priest without disturbing his odd little dance. As the inspector drew nearer, he could hear that Father O'Rourke was making his own music, "Kyrie eleison, Kyrie eleison, Christe eleison," the elderly voice crackled and crooned a spirited version of the acclamation, while he swayed and rocked and clipped away at a rose bush.

The inspector stood and watched this little scene for a moment or two, reluctant to intrude on the old man's oblivion. Finally, he cleared his throat, hoping the priest would notice. When that failed, he called gently to the old man, "Good morning, Father."

The priest startled so, he dropped his clippers. He turned to the voice and nervously ran his hands through his hair. He walked cautiously down the slope of the garden toward Desmond Joyce, worrying his hands as he walked.

"Well now, well, well," he said. "I wondered if you'd be back. Yes I did. I wondered if you'd be back to talk to me again." And Father O'Rourke extended a frail but sincere hand to Desmond Joyce.

"I'm sorry to interrupt you," the inspector offered. But Father O'Rourke only laughed.

"I'm not embarrassed, sir, not embarrassed at all," the priest chuckled. "You're not the first person to catch me singing in my garden. This is a very public thoroughfare."

Taking this as his cue, Desmond Joyce said, "Since this is a public thoroughfare, Father, I would prefer that we go somewhere else to talk."

"Oh, so it's privacy we need, is it?" Father O'Rourke asked. "Well then, let's go to my study, shall we?"

"Lead the way, Father."

Desmond Joyce followed Father O'Rourke along the walk which circled the Doctor Road side of the church, the priest plucking roses and lilacs from their bushes as they walked. Every so often, the inspector could hear the priest hum a few bars of his Kyrie.

Behind the church was the rectory, and as they entered it, the priest very carefully wiped his shoes on an old, frayed rug. He requested that Desmond Joyce do the same.

While the inspector did as he was bidden, Father O'Rourke motioned to the door of his study and invited him to go in and have a seat as soon as his shoes were clean. Then the priest disappeared down a hall, humming his Kyrie a good bit louder as he went.

The study was, like its owner, old and sparse. The furnishings were meager and worn almost to uselessness—a rickety desk and a few unmatched chairs, which were of no more substantial strength than the desk. Desmond Joyce selected the strongest looking chair and cautiously lowered his great body onto the seat. The chair squeaked beneath his weight, but it held him. He sighed gratefully.

He had only a moment to wait. Heralded by a now full-throttle Kyrie, Father O'Rourke marched into the room carrying in his arms an old Arklow pottery vase overflowing with the newly plucked roses and lilacs.

The priest set the vase in the middle of the desk and stepped back a bit to get a full view of his flowers.

"There now, there now," he said, obviously happy with his bouquet. He turned to Desmond Joyce saying, "Our Lord certainly knew what he was doing when he created these beauties." He smiled appreciatively. Then, becoming more serious, he said, "Ah, but you didn't come here to admire my flowers, no you didn't."

"No, I didn't. Please be seated, Father. We may be talking for a while."

"Yes, yes, my son." And Father O'Rourke seated himself in the chair behind the desk.

chapter 40

Inspector Joyce quickly thought about how to question this man. He wanted to be gentle, of course, yet he knew he must be firm in order to elicit the answers he needed. He decided that a slow, soft-spoken but direct approach would be best.

He began, "Father, I need more information about the deceased Major Arthur Fitzgerald." He paused for a moment, then said, "In order to solve this case, I need to know far more about him...you understand?"

Father O'Rourke quickly assured him that he understood perfectly. Then, to Desmond Joyce's surprise, the good Father countered, "But inspector, there is something you must understand. I will happily tell you anything I can. But I cannot...I repeat, cannot...reveal anything that was told to me in the confessional."

"I can understand that you would feel morally obligated to..."

But Father O'Rourke interrupted him. "Oh, yes, yes, yes indeed, I do feel morally obligated to keep a secret what is confessed to me. But more important than that—yes, more important than that—my priestly vows forbid me, absolutely forbid me, to disclose what is told to me in the confessional."

The elderly Father had spoken with all the correctness of a math teacher. His meager frame was now straight and erect.

"If I were to betray a confession, I would have to confess that. There would be repercussions."

Then he relaxed against the back of his chair, his body worn from the simple exertion of making his point. After a few deep breaths, he addressed the inspector again.

"Please," he petitioned, "Please do not ask me to break my vows."

Desmond Joyce was somewhat surprised by the Father's emotional plea.

"Am I correct in assuming that something regarding the major's death was confessed to you?" he asked.

"No, no, not that," the priest said and shook his head back and forth as if dismissing the whole idea.

Desmond Joyce considered this for a few seconds. Then he said, "I believe I can then assume that the major himself confessed something to you. Of course, that must be it. That's why you remember him. It did seem unusual to me that you remembered knowing an army sergeant from a meeting twenty-five years ago. After all, hundreds of soldiers recuperated here. Yes, he must have confessed something to you, some terrible crime that he committed."

Father O'Rourke covered his face with both of his knotty, spindly hands.

"Please do not ask me that."

"Then let me ask you this," Desmond Joyce demanded. "Do you know of some reason why some person or persons could bear such malice toward Major Arthur Fitzgerald that they would want to kill him?"

"Possibly."

The inspector considered this reply.

"Possibly?" he questioned.

"Yes, just possibly."

The two men looked at each other steadily, quietly, for what seemed like a long time. Desmond Joyce broke the silence and launched a more circuitous line of questioning.

"Do you know Mrs. Quinn's guests at Sea View?"

Now Father O'Rourke had to laugh.

"You're not one to be underestimated. No indeed, sir. Well, you might say I know of them, and I've seen them, but I've not had the pleasure of making their acquaintance."

Inspector Joyce smiled indulgently.

"Would you care to explain all that, Father?" he asked.

The priest smiled with a roguish grin.

"Let me just say that Mrs. Frances Houlihan cleans the rectory for me. She was in just a few days ago."

"From what she told you, do you have any particular thoughts about those people?"

This question had an obviously sobering effect on the priest. He closed his eyes, and although he made no audible sound, his lips began moving as though in prayer.

Inspector Joyce noticed that Father O'Rourke's fingers were moving delicately over his rosary. *The Decade of Sorrow?* Desmond Joyce could not bring himself to interrupt the old man's meditation. Thus, there was nothing he could do but wait and hope that the priest didn't intend to say the entire rosary.

He hadn't as long to wait as he had feared, for as soon as Father O'Rourke's fingers left the last bead of that decade, the old man sighed and opened his eyes. He smiled at the inspector.

"Thank you for your patience," he said.

"Would you like me to repeat my question?" Joyce asked.

The priest's expression became pensive. He shook his head.

"No, no. There's no need for that. No need at all," he said softly.

He leaned forward in his chair, resting his elbows on the desk and pressing his fingertips together.

"Actually, sir, my prayer has just now been answered. You see, I want to help you, I really do. Yet I am bound by my vows. Yes indeed, bound. But a way has been revealed to me." He chuckled happily. "I'm going to tell you a story."

chapter 41

Upon seeing the expression on Desmond Joyce's face, the priest assured him, "Oh, don't worry, don't worry, inspector. This is a story you want to hear. But first…"

The priest rose quietly from his chair and walked across the room to an old cupboard. He opened the door to the cupboard and from inside, took out two small glasses and a half-empty bottle of John Power whiskey. He tottered back to the desk where he delicately poured them each a generous measure.

"Slanjte'," they toasted.

Desmond Joyce took a slow, steady mouthful of the excellent blend. He swallowed appreciatively. "Mmmm…" he sighed.

Father O'Rourke delighted in his guest's enjoyment. "There aren't many luxuries in my life. But I think you want to hear the story I promised you, yes? Yes, indeed."

The priest held his glass up to his face and inhaled the whiskey's full aroma. Then he poured a small bit over his tongue, swirled it about expertly and swallowed. He sighed deeply.

"Let me see now, let me see. Where shall I begin? You know, sir, just a few days ago, I gave the Last Rites of the Church to a man who had been murdered—the major, of course. This was not the first time I've oiled the forehead of a murdered man. No, no. Twenty-five years ago, I gave the Last Rites to another man who had been killed. And there could be a connection between those two. Yes, a connection. But I can say no more about that."

"The first victim, twenty-five years ago, was a local man by the name of Seamus O'Byrne. Now Seamus was a sorry kind of fellow. His wife was dead. She had been strange, you know, and ended her own life. God rest her soul. Seamus was left with two young children, a boy and a girl. Now Seamus was a good man at heart, but he liked his Guinness, he did. When he drank a bit extra, he often got into fights."

"One night there were lots of soldiers stealing about town. On leave from the hospital, you know. Anyroad, Seamus got a bit drunk and got into an altercation with a soldier. Later that night, Seamus was found dead in an alley. He had been shot twice, yes twice, with a military-type weapon. Of course, people suspected a soldier, but there was no proof. No witnesses. Everyone had an alibi."

Here the priest's voice trailed off.

Desmond Joyce spoke up, "You knew who the solder was, did you not?"

Painfully, Father O'Rourke admitted that he did. Then he insisted, "Not until later! No indeed, not until much later. But I'll say no more about that."

"No, of course not," Desmond Joyce concurred, but added, "Please tell me about the children."

The father nodded in agreement and began, "As I said, there was a boy and a girl. At the time the boy was... oh, let me see...I would guess maybe fifteen years old. Yes, fifteen."

The inspector reacted in surprise. "As old as that?" he asked. "Fifteen is practically a grown man! I thought you said children!"

"He was a child in many ways—wild, undisciplined, full of himself," the priest asserted. "But he was older than his time, too. With his poor ma being sick all of her life and his da being a drinker, the poor lad—Sean, his name was... funny how the name just came to me...Sean was the grown-up in the family. Yet, when his da died, he cried like a baby, yes he did. His little sister had to comfort him."

"The girl was younger?"

"She was that," the father answered. "Moira, that was her name, might have been about ten years old when Seamus O'Byrne met his death."

"And what sort of child was this Moira O'Byrne?"

"Much like her ma, I'm afraid. Much like her ma," The priest said sadly.

"In what way?"

"Well, as I told you, the mother was a poor, sad creature. Not friendly, not pleasant. An angry woman. Always ready to argue with God, then suffer and cry. Rumor had it that Seamus married her out of pity. Anyroad, she was able to talk the local chemist into selling her small amounts of sleeping medicine over a few months' time. She took the whole amount one night. Never woke up again. Sad, sad."

The priest paused for another sip of whiskey. After an appreciative sigh, he continued, "So little Moira was very much like her ma. Never showed fear or caution, only anger. She kept away from other children."

"You seem to remember a great many details about these children, Father," Desmond Joyce commented.

"Well, I guess I should. Yes, I should," the priest agreed. "After the da was killed, I brought them here to live with me temporarily. I found a new home for them."

"Is that right?" Desmond Joyce asked. He was beginning to wonder about the pertinence of Father O'Rourke's story. His question had been asked without much enthusiasm.

The priest smiled slyly. "Wouldn't you be interested in knowing where they went?" he teased.

Desmond Joyce showed renewed interest.

"This is important information then?"

"Oh my, my!" the priest chastised. "I hope you don't think these are the ramblings of a senile old man. You see, inspector, Sean and Moira were sent to their mother's sister in Scotland. I kept in touch with Mrs. Balfour for a few years. The Balfours adopted young Moira..."

"And called her by her English name, Mary! Mary Balfour!" the inspector was now very interested.

"Yes, yes," Father O'Rourke confirmed. "But the boy ran off soon after reaching Scotland. Headed for America, Mrs. Balfour thought."

"Sean, Sean?" The inspector was thinking aloud. "In English, it's John."

"Of course. We both know that Sean translates to John."

"You know where John and Mary are now, don't you?" Desmond Joyce stated without a trace of doubt.

"I know nothing for certain, nothing at all," he denied. "I only consider what's possible. But that's not the end of my story."

At last Desmond Joyce could see where this tale was leading. He already knew something of the backgrounds of John Murphy and Mary MacGregor, nee Sean O'Byrne and Moira O'Byrne. Emma Quinn and Frances Houlihan suspected there was a connection between those red-haired people, but they hadn't been able to put a label to the connection. Now the inspector had the label. John and Mary were brother and sister! He asked the priest to continue his story.

chapter 42

The priest stared at his hands on the old wooden table for just a few seconds, and then began.

"Yes, I'm not finished telling this story. A certain soldier kept in touch with me for a few years after the war. One time in particular, he wrote me a very troubled letter, very troubled indeed. He had been left guardian for a young nephew and niece. They were not brother and sister, you understand. No, they were cousins, each a child of a sister of the solder, but different sisters. Am I making myself clear?"

The inspector again wondered where this story was going. Apparently, Father O'Rourke was focused more on the soldier than on Murphy and MacGregor. He surmised, though, that the solder in question was the same one suspected of murdering Seamus O'Byrne. He needed to hear more

"Yes." Desmond Joyce was amused at the priest's perplexed expression. "I understand their relationship. Please go on."

"Well, in his letter, this certain soldier said he was very worried about these children, very worried indeed. He was trying to do his best…felt it was his duty to raise these children in the church. He asked for my prayers for them and his effort."

Father O'Rourke breathed deeply. The priest sat thinking, trying to decide how much more to reveal. He stared into his whisky glass, unseeing, for some time. Then he continued, "Inspector, in his letter, he called the girl a 'saucy wench.' He said her chest was 'budding,' and that her hips were becoming round."

The priest paused briefly and then continued, "Inspector, she was only eleven years old. I feared that he… well, never mind."

"Anyway, I knew many things about this soldier, which in my opinion, made him an unsuitable guardian. I sent him a letter in the next post and told him I'd get the children relocated. I also rang up the vicar of the local parish and asked him to intervene. He did just that, yes he did. The appropriate agency was consulted, and the children were removed straight away."

The two men sat in silence, Inspector Joyce wondering what the significance of these children was, and Father O'Rourke hoping that he hadn't betrayed a confession.

Finally, Desmond Joyce asked, "What were the children's names?"

The priest shook his head. "I don't recall," he said. "And I don't think it's important who they were. The situation was handled well, yes it was."

The father's focus drifted for a moment, but he quickly gathered his thoughts again and continued. "My point, sir…my point is that this soldier had visited me in the confessional many years before. His sins were many and serious, especially crimes against girls and young women.

A British soldier he was, but he stayed in Ireland after the war. In a way, I think he was asking for more than help. He was asking for absolution. I thought he was asking me to stop him from committing another crime, yes I did. But his slate wasn't clean, no indeed, and I told him so. You know there are some sins that you have to make restitution for before you receive complete absolution."

The inspector made no reply at first. The father was also silent, having said all he could. After some time, Desmond Joyce shifted his weight. The chair creaked but continued to hold.

"Father O'Rourke," he said, "Your stories are amazing. I believe you told them to me because you knew I'd recognize the characters involved, and I do."

"Perhaps, perhaps," the priest replied, innocently.

"The soldier, of course, was Arthur Fitzgerald."

"You can understand I can neither confirm nor deny that."

"Sean and Moira must be John Murphy and Mary Balfour. It would be too much of a coincidence otherwise."

The priest shrugged his shoulders.

"You know, sir, that my vows absolutely forbid me from saying yes or no. Absolutely."

But Desmond Joyce knew he was correct.

"Sean and Moira, or John and Mary, I bet they were red-haired."

Father O'Rourke nodded his head slowly, as though weighed down by this truth. The inspector observed this and said, "Please don't feel guilty. I can have all this information confirmed at Dublin Castle. No one will ever know you've told me anything."

The priest responded…however, more to himself than aloud…"But I know."

The chief inspector stood up from his chair but made no motion toward leaving. He stretched a bit, working some stiffness out of his knees and back. Then he said, "Here's what I believe: I believe that Sean O'Byrne is now the man I know as John Murphy, and Moira O'Byrne became Mary Balfour MacGregor. I'm sure they're not here by chance. They managed somehow over the years to keep in touch. And I'm sure they managed to learn the name of the British soldier who killed their father."

"John Murphy knew a couple by the name of Burke who stayed with Emma Quinn a few years ago and met up with Arthur Fitzgerald. Murphy contacted his sister, and they arranged to meet here in Howth when Fitzgerald would be here. I don't know for certain what they planned for the major. Maybe murder, maybe not."

Desmond Joyce reached across the desk and shook the priest's hand, saying, "I won't take any more of your time today, Father. I appreciate your help."

But before the inspector left the study, he thought of another area of investigation where Father O'Rourke could be of assistance.

He asked, "Father, do you have a bit more time for me? I've just now…"

He didn't finish his statement, for the priest was smiling and pointing Joyce back to his chair.

"Thank you," the inspector offered.

"Ask anything, sir. Anything at all." The priest was magnanimous.

"A bit more John Power?"

Desmond Joyce declined graciously, but said, "I need to ask you about Emma and Tommy Quinn. Tell me what you can about them."

The priest complied. "There's nothing bad to say about Emma Quinn. She was a beautiful young girl when she and Tommy moved here. Newlywed, they were. Tommy got work at the brewery."

He stopped for a bit, obviously thinking about what he wanted to say next.

"Emma was raised by the Magdalens, dropped off with them as a baby. No family that she knew of. Anyroad, Emma was full of hope. She wanted children and made a good home waiting for them. None came."

"Tommy was different. A wise-guy, a joker, if you know what I mean. Not responsible. It's a wonder the brewery kept him on these past few years. He must have missed a lot of work—he's a big drinker, you know. Yes he is."

Desmond Joyce didn't interrupt as Father O'Rourke again paused to collect his thoughts.

When the father was ready to continue, he said, "Over the years, I could see the change in Emma, yes I could. Her hopeful attitude just went away. She never complained, at least not to me, no she didn't. But she deserved better than she married."

None of this information was news to Inspector Joyce. Boyle, Curry and Frances Houlihan had told him essentially the same thing. Before he could ask another question, though, the priest added, "Inspector, take a good look at Tommy Quinn."

The inspector's eyebrows raised.

"Why do you say that?" he asked.

Father O'Rourke shrugged his shoulders and said, "I think he's a deceitful man, yes I do. He's not to be trusted. I've seen him with some thugs, men not from Howth. And with his heavy drinking and missing work…well, I think he's a sick, desperate man."

Desmond Joyce arose to leave.

"You've been a tremendous help, Father," he said. "I'm in your debt."

This time, he left.

chapter 43

Walking from St. Michael Church to the Howth Garda Station gave Desmond Joyce an opportunity to consider all he had learned about Major Arthur Fitzgerald, his murder and the people involved.

The major's name and history were well known to Inspector Joyce. Fitzgerald had been known to Interpol for many years, for he'd been acting as a double agent. Not only did he transport money to his various contacts in Donegal, he also brought back information about IRA activities to sell to someone 'high up' in British Intelligence. That his information was occasionally wrong or often not precise, had red-flagged his name.

Arthur Fitzgerald's wartime record was seemingly honorable. He had been a pilot for the British Army. Ireland was neutral during World War II; nevertheless, the country had two thousand miles of coastline to protect against invasion by the powerful German navy.

At the start of the war, Ireland had about six thousand poorly armed soldiers, a miniscule air force and no navy at all. Winston Churchill realized that Ireland would need help protecting its coastline. Certainly, if German troops arrived in Ireland, it would be easy for them to invade Britain. In

1943, Churchill sent a squadron of Hawker Hurricanes to Ireland to provide coastal security. Arthur Fitzgerald flew one of those planes.

As the squadron approached the Irish coast, it was attacked by Luftwaffe planes. Fitzgerald's plane was damaged and made a crippled landing just north of Dublin Bay. Fitzgerald was badly, but not fatally, injured and taken to the hospital in Howth.

After he was well enough to leave the hospital, the major stayed on in Howth in a convalescent home. He still required daily therapy and went to the hospital every morning. The rest of his time was completely free for taking long drives, allegedly to visit his distant relatives near the border of Ulster, Northern Ireland.

He left Howth, moving to Waterford in 1944. Then in 1948 he returned to England. His activities had been followed surreptitiously since his discharge from the British Army in 1950. British Intelligence and its Irish counterpart had cooperated with information about the man. Chief Inspector Desmond Joyce had been responsible for logging his movements while he was in County Dublin. The file on the major was thick indeed.

And who in Howth knew the major? Desmond Joyce mentally reviewed the people he considered to be suspects. *Emma Quinn was certainly not a suspect. Not Emma, so lovely and warm. Not her.*

Frances Houlihan? Good God, no. Preposterous. She hadn't the wit for it.

No apparent connection to Jean Blair or Gwillam Morgan. Morgan's juvenile arrest had been expunged from the records. Jean Blair had apparently never so much as jay-walked.

Father O'Rourke? Utterly impossible, not because of his vocation, but because of his frailty.

That leaves Mary MacGregor and John Murphy. They certainly had motive, but did they really have the opportunity? The coroner determined the time of death to be between seven a.m. and seven-thirty a.m. on June fifth. Surely Emma Quinn would have known if those two red-haired people had stolen away from her home in the wee hours of the morning.

He remembered Emma saying that both Murphy and Mrs. MacGregor had been at breakfast on the morning when the major's dead body was discovered. That meant that by eight o'clock that morning, both people were with the other guests at Sea View.

I don't know, he thought. *I don't know if those two could have left Sea View that morning and returned without being seen.*

Where does that leave me? he wondered. *Who's left?*

He knew there was always the possibility of an IRA operative doing the killing. They probably found out about the major's double-dealing and decided to eliminate him. But Desmond Joyce knew that discovering the identity of this operative would be impossible. The IRA was extremely secretive. Swift and painful death came to traitors to their cause.

No, the clue lay somewhere in what Father O'Rourke had told him, he was certain of that. He was certain of John Murphy's and Mary MacGregor's relationship. All the details could be proven through legal channels, but he suspected that, confronted with the truth, they wouldn't deny it. They would have been old enough when their father was killed to find out who killed him. They obviously maintained contact with each other over the years.

But the bottom line was, could they have snuck out and back into Sea View without being seen by Jean Blair? Emma Quinn? They never could have escaped Kitty Murphy, of that he was certain.

He was missing something.

Of course!

He stopped dead in his tracks. *I've had the pieces to this puzzle for two days. I didn't put them together until just this minute!*

The man who helped the major into the Ford on Tuesday after Mass! The major was abducted! That was the man, the killer! The man shot the major and dumped his body in the alley behind the Royal. Murphy and MacGregor could have hired this man. Or he could have been acting on his own. Or was he IRA? Or British Intelligence? This unknown man had all the answers.

Was this unknown man the same person who had attacked Emma? They had to be the same person, the major's murderer and Emma's would-be strangler.

By now he had reached and entered the Howth Garda Station. As he walked past the matronly receptionist, he ordered her to ring up Emma Quinn for him. He was intentionally gruff and terse. He had no time for her silliness. He went into a private office to await the call. In just a couple minutes, the phone rang. It was Emma on the line.

"It's good to hear your voice," Desmond Joyce offered.

"You too," she replied softly.

His breath caught as he heard her honesty.

"Emma," he said, "You've become very important to me." There was more emotion in his voice than he could control.

"Oh, I...don't...know...what...to...do." It was difficult for her to talk for she had begun to cry.

"I don't want you to be upset," he said, mustering more self-control.

"Actually, I called to see if your husband is home. You know, Emma, I've had my men contact the brewery where Tom works—or worked. He hasn't been there in weeks. Did you know that?"

She paused, and then answered with resignation, "I did not..."

"Do you know where he is now?" he asked.

"As a matter of fact, I do. Dr. Hernon rang me just a bit ago. Tommy's back in the hospital as of this morning."

"And how long will he stay this time," he wondered aloud.

But Emma answered his question, "I'm to get directly there. Tommy's had a stomach hemorrhage this morning. Dr. Hernon doesn't think he'll live long."

She said the words simply, no sadness, no self pity nor tremor in her voice. This is what is to be—that's all.

"You're alright?" he asked, but he knew she was.

"I am."

"I'll come round and drive you there," he offered.

She refused his offer. "It wouldn't do," she said.

"Quite right, of course."

He knew she was correct. He added, though, "I'll send Boyle to take you. But I'll come along in a bit."

"Yes, please."

Hanging up the phone, he paused, thinking about Tommy Quinn's predicted demise.

Emma will be free, he thought. *After a respectable time of mourning, we could be together.*

chapter 44

Like a thunderbolt, a realization came to him! Tommy Quinn! Father O'Rourke had practically told him so! The car that drove up from the pier—it stopped for the major. A thin man got out of the car and pulled the major into it! A thin man who reminded Father O'Rourke of Tommy Quinn! The fishermen on the pier had observed the major talking privately to a man who resembled Tommy. And the priest called Tommy deceitful…said he associated with thugs that weren't local men.

"Boyle!" he yelled at the top of his voice.

Boyle reacted instantly.

"Sir?"

"Get to Sea View! Collect Emma Quinn and get her to the hospital! Her husband is critical! Hurry!"

"Curry!"

"Sir?" The response was immediate.

"Get a car! We've got to get to the hospital before Tommy Quinn dies!"

But the frazzled receptionist commanded the inspector's attention.

"Wait!" she demanded.

Desmond Joyce almost bowled her over, but she shouted, "Stop!" and blocked the door with her ample female body.

"What the Hell?" was all the inspector had time to say before he shoved her aside and hurried from the building. He faintly heard the woman calling, "Sergeant Malloy wants to talk to you!"

Desmond Joyce briefly turned and called back, "Tell him to go fishing!"

Curry easily pulled the vehicle out into the traffic, the claxon blaring its ear-piercing alarm. Other autos quickly moved aside for the official car.

Curry had to know.

"Sir, what's happening? Why do you care if Tommy Quinn dies?"

"Because I believe that Mrs. Quinn's husband killed the major, but I don't have proof. Thus, I need him to confess."

Desmond Joyce's voice was steel.

Curry had no comment.

chapter 45

The hospital room had only one bed and Tommy Quinn lay in that bed, his life being sustained by the tubes going into this body.

There was a glass bottle that hung upside down from a pole. The bottle contained a clear solution that dripped into plastic tubing. The tubing entered a vein in Tommy's left arm. A bottle containing blood was also hanging from the same pole. The blood was dripping fast into its own tubing, which connected in the "Y" with the other before it reached his arm.

Emerging from Tommy's right nostril was a large, orange rubber tube. The tube reached from his stomach, up and out his nose to a suction machine positioned by his bed. This tube carried blood—Tommy's blood—up from his stomach to a vacuum bottle in the machine. Tommy appeared to be losing blood as fast, if not faster, than he was receiving it.

Tommy's head and chest were enclosed in a huge, clear plastic tent. Green tanks of oxygen stood behind the head of his bed and filled the tent with highly oxygenated air. Even so, he seemed to be laboring for his breath.

Inspector Joyce entered the room and joined Emma and Dr. Hernon at Tommy's bedside. He stared at Tommy, who had barely any life left in him. Tommy's eyes were closed. His skin was gray against the white sheets he lay upon.

The inspector's instinct was to reach over and put an arm around Emma, but his sense of propriety prevailed. Instead, he asked of Dr. Hernon, "Can he talk?"

"He hasn't as of yet," the doctor replied.

"Has Father O'Rourke been called?"

"Yes. He'll be here straight away."

Desmond Joyce turned to Emma and said, "I want you to wake him up. Call his name, take his hand and squeeze it...anything. Just get him awake."

Puzzled, Emma looked from the inspector to Dr. Hernon.

"Can he still wake up?" she asked.

The doctor reassured her, "Just do whatever the inspector says."

Emma took her husband's right hand.

"Tom? Tom? Tommy!" she said, massaging his hand gently.

"Tom!" This time she was more insistent, but there was no response.

"Doctor, I need him awake!" demanded Inspector Joyce.

Dr. Hernon walked to the foot of the bed. Pulling the sheets off Tommy's feet, he lifted one foot and held it securely in his left hand. With his right hand, he took some keys from his pocket, selected the largest one and dragged it firmly up the sole of Tommy's foot.

The response was immediate: the leg jerk, the attempt to withdraw the foot. However, no sound came from the man. There was a brief indication of a frown on Tommy's face, but his eyes remained closed.

"Do it again," Inspector Joyce demanded. "Keep doing it until he wakes up!"

The doctor took hold of Tommy's right foot this time. Otherwise, the procedure was the same. The reaction was immediate and a bit stronger than before. There was even a moan this time.

At the doctor's third attempt, Desmond Joyce pulled the plastic tent loose from the sheets. When the key annoyed Tommy to the point of his leg jerking, the inspector put his face right down into the patient's, and commanded, "TOM, WAKE UP!" He shook the man's puny shoulders and demanded again, "TOM, I SAID WAKE UP!"

Up from the arms of Morpheus rose Tommy Quinn's life. His head tossed. His untethered right arm scratched at the air. He moaned. He opened his eyes and, looking directly at Desmond Joyce, swore, "What the bloody hell…"

"Just as I thought." The inspector was smug.

"You stay awake, man!" he commanded. "You have some talking to do."

As Desmond Joyce was speaking, there was a timid rap on the door. Dr. Hernon opened the door to find Father

O'Rourke waiting there. The doctor motioned for him to come in.

"By my faith," he said, a perplexed expression on his face. "I thought I heard some loud voices in here, yes I did."

He chuckled as he raised his hand to the top of his head and scratched his near-barren scalp.

The inspector beckoned for the priest to come by him, near Tommy's bedside.

"Father," he said, "Both you and I are going to hear Tommy's final confession. Then you give him the Last Rites."

Evidently, Tommy Quinn was both awake enough and alert enough to understand what was said, for he protested immediately.

"Last Rites my arse…"

A menacing stare from Desmond Joyce stopped him.

The inspector politely asked Emma and the doctor to leave the room. "The good father and I need to talk to Tommy alone, probably for just a few minutes"

"You'll call me if he changes?" Dr. Hernon asked.

"You have my word," Desmond Joyce promised.

Then, touching Emma's shoulders gently, he turned her toward the door.

"I won't cause him any stress," he assured her. "He has only to tell me the truth and I'll leave him in Father O'Rourke's hands."

It was obvious that Emma didn't understand the meaning of his words, but when her eyes made contact with his, she knew she could trust this good man.

She and Dr. Hernon left the room.

Astutely, the priest stepped back from Tommy's bed, allowing Desmond Joyce to have the dying man's full attention.

"Tom," he began, "It's very important that you tell me the truth."

"Kiss my arse," was Tommy's reply.

"Tommy, my man, I can hurt you in ways that will never show."

"But you promised Em…"

"She'll never know."

At this point, Father O'Rourke cleared his throat. "Ahem" was the sound he made. Both the patient and Desmond Joyce were distracted by this sound. The priest then stepped closer to the head of the bed. He nudged the inspector aside a bit and chastised him saying, "There's no need for threats, inspector. No need at all."

Chapter 46

Father O'Rourke addressed Tommy.

"I don't know what it is that this man wants you to say. By my faith, I don't. But, Tommy…"

Here the priest's voice softened. He took the dying man's right hand in both of his hands and held it close to his own chest. The priest was looking at the wasted, guarded, alcoholic man with genuine respect and love. Desmond Joyce observed this and kept a discrete distance back. Father O'Rourke leaned closer to the patient, saying, "Tommy, it's not too late to ask for forgiveness. You're dying now, and God is watching over you very closely. He wants to take you home with Him, yes he does. But you need to confess, son. Confess, Tommy, so I can give you God's absolution and free your soul."

The priest's eyes filled with tears.

"Please, Tommy."

There followed a silence that was solemn. The priest's heart-felt sadness was touching. In a raspy, thin voice, Tommy Quinn said, "I killed him."

Tommy's strength was ebbing. His skin became even paler, and a cyanotic hue appeared under his eyes and around his mouth.

From a position a few feet away, Desmond Joyce interjected, "Tell us the name of the man you killed."

Tommy whispered, "Fitzgerald." His eyes were closed now. His breathing became irregular.

"Don't die yet!" the inspector commanded. "Tell us why you killed him!"

The faintest snicker came from Tommy Quinn, but he obeyed the inspector.

"I...was paid," he said, his voice barely audible.

"By whom?" Desmond Joyce thundered.

"Not sure...who...they...are. Pay...me...cash... Dangerous." Tommy gasped with each word.

"Who was your contact?" Desmond Joyce demanded.

"Different...each...time...No...names."

"But why?" questioned Father O'Rourke, a good deal more gently than the chief inspector would have done.

Tommy tried to swallow. The orange tube in the back of his throat was obviously irritating. His mouth was too dry, and he was too weak.

Father O'Rourke offered to put a spoonful of water in Tommy's mouth, but the inspector stopped him.

"He might choke," Desmond Joyce said. "We'll let Dr. Hernon do that, as soon as Tommy tells us what we need to know."

So Father O'Rourke continued gently, lovingly, with his questioning.

"Why did you kill him, Tommy?"

"Needed…money…Lost…job…weeks…ago." Each word left him breathless.

"Who paid you?"

Tommy shook his head, a movement so small it could easily have been missed.

"Don't…know…name. Radicals…IRA."

Father O'Rourke turned to Inspector Joyce and begged, "How much more, sir? How much more? He's nearly gone."

Desmond Joyce touched the priest lightly on the arm.

"Let me finish," he said.

"Tommy," he spoke, and saw a flicker of a sneer on the man's face.

"Just answer yes or no, understand?"

The inspector interpreted the lack of a sneer this time as Tommy's willingness to continue.

"On the night after the major's killing, someone put on your wife's flowered robe and lured her into the bathroom. When she went in, this person choked her with the belt from the robe until she passed out. I believe you did this. Am I correct?"

Tommy whispered, "Yes."

The inspector waited, and then asked, "You intended to kill your own wife?"

Tommy's lips formed the word 'no'. He summoned more strength and added, "Needed...get...away."

There seemed nothing more to add or say. Desmond Joyce just stood and looked at the dying man, not knowing what to feel. Pity seemed too good an emotion for Tommy Quinn, and yet the inspector was experiencing something like pity for this wretched man. Or was it simply an acknowledgement of his personhood? It didn't matter in the end.

He turned to go.

"Wait."

The voice from the man in the bed was so feeble, the inspector wasn't sure he had heard anything at all. He turned back to the bed and saw that Tommy's eyes were open. Desmond Joyce moved closer.

With a sound less than a whisper, Tommy mouthed the words, "Take...care...of...Emma."

His eyes closed. His breathing became shallower.

Father O'Rourke looked up into the face of the chief inspector with incredibly sad eyes.

"You leave now," he said. "He needs a blessing."

chapter 47

Outside the hospital room, Emma, the doctor, Boyle and Curry were waiting. As Desmond Joyce stepped from the room, Emma and the doctor approached him. They both focused on his face, looking for answers to questions they didn't dare ask.

The inspector regarded them both, and then turned to Emma. With an unmistakable tenderness in his voice, he said, "I have a lot to tell you."

Not turning from her, he said to the doctor, "Tommy needs you now, Hernon."

He put his arm around Emma's shoulders and bid her walk down the corridor with him. Passing Boyle and Curry, he ordered them to remain where they were. He ignored the way they were staring at him and Emma.

When they had walked about thirty feet, he motioned her over to a nearby bench. They sat, not too close together, but close enough that their conversation could be held quietly and not overheard by passers-by.

"Is he dead?" Emma asked with composure and calm.

Desmond Joyce thought that he had never known a woman as fine as Emma. He admired her peacefulness as much as he desired her loveliness. He answered, "He was just barely alive when I left the room." He added, "If you need to say goodbye to him, we'd better go back straight away."

Without a moment's hesitation, she said, "No, I don't think I do. You know we've not been close in years. I don't think I'll miss him much at all, God forgive me."

The inspector took her hands in his. "He asked me to take care of you," he told her. "I intend to do that."

"So, he thought of me after all," she smiled.

"Yes. But there are things you must be told…things about Tommy."

She didn't reply, but from the expression on her face, he knew he should continue.

"Emma, Tommy made his confession to Father O'Rourke and to me. He confessed to the murder of Major Arthur Fitzgerald."

"That's impossible!" Emma was shocked. "Why would he say that? What reason would he have to kill the major?"

"He was paid to do it. And it was Tommy who tried to strangle you."

She shook her head in disbelief, saying, "No, no. Why?" Her eyes filled with horror at the truth of what he was telling her.

She looked directly into Desmond Joyce's eyes and said, "Then he really didn't care about me at all either, did he?"

Desmond Joyce had no answer for that question. He kept silent, allowing her time for disappointment to sink in.

At last she asked, "Who paid him to kill the major?"

The inspector had to tell her that Tommy's answer to that question was woefully incomplete.

"There'll be more investigating into that murder and an investigation of Tommy, specifically," he advised her. "You'll no doubt be questioned about him."

"I feel I've been married to a complete stranger," she admitted. Then she demanded, "But why try to kill me? I didn't know anything more about the major than he did." With bewilderment filling her eyes, she asked, "Did he hate me?"

"I don't think so," he said. And he realized the irony of his conversation. He was defending a man who had assaulted his own wife, the woman, he, himself, loved.

He moved slightly closer to her and gently squeezed her hands.

"Emma," he explained, "I think he just needed to get out of the house, and you were in the way. He said he didn't intend to kill you or even hurt you."

She collected her thoughts for a moment and then turned abruptly to him.

"I should have known it was Tommy! He's the only one who knew how to get into the house without me seeing him!"

chapter 48

It was Desmond Joyce's turn to be puzzled.

"How's that?" he questioned. "There's a secret way in and out of your home?"

"In, not out," she answered. "Above my bedroom is a small attic. The access to it is in my closet. But the closet ceiling is so high you need a ladder to reach it."

"And from outdoors?"

"From outdoors, a thin person could scale the trellises and ivy to the attic window. It's a small window, but Tommy was skinny enough to get in. He must have dropped down from the attic while I was still downstairs. Otherwise, I would have heard him."

"He hid in the closet until he was sure no one would be out in the hall on their way to the loo," the inspector speculated. "He put on your robe and shower cap just in case."

"And ducked into the bathroom."

They were finishing each other's sentences. They both recognized the irony of this—that two people known to each other for just a few days could share the same thoughts.

"You know, if the faucet hadn't been dripping, you might have walked right past the bathroom and not been assaulted," Desmond Joyce guessed.

She shook her head. "You're forgetting something. The light bulb in the ceiling fixture was loosened. It wouldn't come on. He did that deliberately. And I think he loosened the tap deliberately, too. He knew I'd hear the dripping."

"You're right, and he couldn't count on hiding for too long in the closet."

Emma lowered her head briefly. Then she raised her face and made mesmerizing eye contact with Desmond Joyce.

"As I said," she told him, "I don't think I'll miss him much at all."

"Well, here comes a couple of familiar men," the inspector stated as he acknowledged the doctor and priest approaching them.

"Does the doctor know about Tommy?" she asked, again having achieved the composure that was so admirable in Desmond Joyce's eyes. They rose from their seats as the two men came nearer.

Father O'Rourke extended his arms to Emma, pulled her close and held her like a daughter.

"It's over, Emma," he said comfortingly. "Tommy made his confession and received absolution. He received the final sacrament. His soul will go to God."

"Thank you, Father," she answered. Then she added, "I think we have to plan a wake and a funeral."

"If you're going home how, I'll send Boyle and Curry on ahead of you," Desmond Joyce stated, and he beckoned for the two garda to come closer.

"Gentlemen, I need you to go to Mrs. Quinn's house. Tell her guests that they will need to settle their accounts with her. They may prepare to leave, but they're to remain at Sea View until I get there."

As he was saying this, he looked at Emma in a questioning way, as though asking her permission. "Yes?" he asked.

"Yes," she agreed.

That Boyle and Curry were completely confused was obvious by the expression on their faces.

"I beg your pardon, gentlemen," the inspector said expansively. "Everyone knows but you, it seems."

In a quieter tone, he continued, "Tommy Quinn confessed to the murder of Major Arthur Fitzgerald."

Office Boyle lifted his cap, scratched his head and said, "Well, I'll be!" While Curry smiled, saying, "Good work, inspector."

Father O'Rourke rose to the occasion and, gathering the little group, urged them toward the hospital exit.

"Come along, everybody, come along," he chuckled. "I think I can answer some of your questions."

"Wait!" Emma declared and asked everyone present, "You were suspicious of my guests. None of them were involved at all?"

"I have the answer to that one," the priest assured them agreeably. "Come along."

chapter 49

We're like a caravan coming to my house, Emma thought. She and Father O'Rourke arrived in his poor, dilapidated Volkswagen, just behind the garda. Desmond Joyce pulled the squad car in parking directly behind them, and she was relieved to see him. She could count on him to take charge of coping with the myriad questions her guests would ask.

As Emma and the priest left his car, she could see Boyle and Curry at the door of Sea View, ordering the guests back into the house. Father O'Rourke took her by the arm saying, "Those folks are ready to pounce, yes they are. Let's wait a wee bit and let Inspector Joyce go in first."

But Emma was distracted by a ghostly apparition running up the street. As it got nearer, Emma recognized the form. It was Francie Houlihan, coming closer and closer, with no sign of stopping. She nearly collided with Emma. She would have, but Desmond Joyce extended one arm and stopped her in mid-stride.

Francie was panting and gasping. The inspector was trying not to laugh at her, but Emma could hear the amusement in his voice.

"Mrs. Houlihan, Mrs. Houlihan. What is your hurry?" he asked, suppressing a chuckle.

Impatiently, Francie pushed his arm away and demanded, "What the H-E-double toothpicks is goin' on 'ere?"

Desmond Joyce turned her squarely to him.

"Please listen to me," he directed. "If you will wait here with Emma for a short while, everything will be explained to you."

Then, addressing Emma, he said, "I'm going in the house now. Give me five minutes, all three of you, and then come in. Come to the parlor."

Emma watched him walk away. She knew she loved him. But she had loved Tommy once upon a time, hadn't she? The difference between the two men was like night and day. Tommy had been a daredevil as a young man, and she'd found him exciting. She couldn't have known twenty years ago that the exciting rogue she married was really an irresponsible alcoholic.

But this man, bigger than life, full of authority and power, was a presence without equal. She felt more of a woman just standing beside him. When their eyes met, she breathed faster. Her face flushed. Her breasts swelled against the fabric of her clothes.

Her thoughts were interrupted by Francie, coarsely shouting, "Dammit, Em! What's goin' on!"

"Tommy died," Emma said quietly.

"Did th' inspector kill 'im?" Francie was agog.

Father O'Rourke came to the rescue.

"No one killed Tommy, no one at all. He died at the hospital—properly shriven—of natural causes, yes he did."

Francie exhaled in a long, noisy, "Whoooooo!"

Her face brightened as a thought occurred to her.

"That means yer free, Em…"

Emma stopped her friend before she could say anymore.

"Hush," she said. "There's a lot more you don't know. It was Tommy that killed the major."

"OH MY GAWD!" the woman exclaimed. Then she added, "That don't make any sense."

Father O'Rourke took each woman by the arm, saying, "Desmond Joyce has the answers. Let's go in and hear what he has to say."

In the parlor sat John and Kitty Murphy, Mary MacGregor, Jean Blair and Gwillam Morgan. No one was talking. They waited quietly, all eyes on Desmond Joyce.

The inspector was seated just inside the door of the room. He rose from his chair as Emma entered. Touching her shoulders, he said softly, "I've had Boyle and Curry bring in some of your chairs from the dining room. I hope that's alright?"

She leaned a bit closer to him and smiled into his eyes. Words weren't necessary.

At his invitation, she, Francie and the priest took seats. Emma was careful to position herself away from the direct stares of her guests. She didn't know how much Desmond Joyce was going to reveal, and she didn't want to be where people would gawk at her. She did trust that he would be as judicious as possible.

He began. Standing up, moving slowly about the room, looking directly at all assembled there, he said, Thank you all for coming. You've been waiting patiently, and now I have some information for you."

"First, let me inform you that Mrs. Quinn's husband died this afternoon. You may express your condolences to Mrs. Quinn a bit later.

"As to the murder of Major Fitzgerald—it's a far more involved situation than any of you knew. At first I suspected you, Mr. Murphy, and you, Mrs. MacGregor. You both know why."

John Murphy colored hotly.

"What do you know?" he demanded of the inspector.

Desmond Joyce motioned to the priest and asked, "Would you care to tell them, Father?"

The old man smiled benevolently.

"John, Mary," he addressed them, "You were Sean and Moira when I sent you to live with your aunt in Edinburgh. It's a long time ago, long indeed, but I'd have known you anywhere."

Gwillam Morgan looked puzzled. Jean Blair mirrored his expression.

Frances Houlihan hadn't the least idea of what was going on, but Emma did. She understood immediately what Desmond Joyce and the priest were saying.

Kitty Murphy was infuriated. She turned sharply in her chair, facing her husband, and charged, "John! What are they talking about?"

The inspector added, "John, Mary, if you don't mind, tell us your story."

"I'll start, John," Mary offered. "Mrs. Murphy, you and I are sisters-in-law. John is my brother."

"I never told you," John said to his wife. "Mary and I made a pact, to never reveal our secret."

This time, Francie jumped in.

"Well, that's clear as mud."

Desmond Joyce interjected, "Let me clear things up. If I'm mistaken about anything, just stop me. John and Mary were born Sean and Moira O'Byrne right here in Howth. Their mother died when they were quite young. Twenty-five years ago, when there were injured soldiers here, their father, one Seamus O'Byrne, was murdered with an army pistol. You two…" he said, indicating John and Mary, "…thought you knew who the murderer was. Being minor children and orphaned, you couldn't stay here alone. Father O'Rourke contacted your aunt in Edinburgh, and she agreed to take you in. You went there. But, John, you didn't stay. Why?"

"Just too angry, I guess. There was nothing for me in Scotland, so I hopped a freighter and made my way to the U.S.A. There I obtained false ID, lied about my age, worked here and there until I was old enough to get on the New York City police force."

"But you and your sister managed to keep in touch, I assume by letter. How did you do it?" the inspector asked.

Mary answered, "John got a post office box. I sent his letters there. He wrote to me at my aunt's. She knew I got letters from him, but she never tried to pry. She said that as long as the letters kept coming, she knew he was alive and, hopefully, alright."

Kitty was having a very hard time fathoming all of this.

"I feel insulted," she voiced. "In fifteen years of marriage, you've kept this secret from me!"

Looking his wife squarely in the eye, he stated, "With good reason, Kitty."

Chapter 50

The inspector interrupted them.

"While we're focused on you, Mrs. Murphy…"

"ON ME?" she screeched, obviously frightened.

"Now, now," Desmond Joyce spoke in a soothing voice. "I just need you to verify some information for me. The truth, please. Where are your parents, your birth parents?"

A very different Kitty first looked at her husband, and then answered Inspector Joyce.

"My parents lived in Waterford. They're deceased now. I was raised by my mother's sister and her husband in Brooklyn."

The inspector studied her and saw a greatly subdued woman. He was sure she knew where his questions would lead.

"Why were you the one sent away? I believe your mother gave birth to two more children after you."

The look on John Murphy's face was one of confusion. He turned to his wife asking, "What's going on here?"

He looked at Kitty, then Desmond Joyce, then back to her, waiting for an answer.

Kitty asked her husband to be patient. Then she said to the inspector, "Why don't you just tell my story? You know what happened."

"As you wish," Inspector Joyce agreed. "I've checked the birth records in Waterford—yes, I knew that fact. The passport bureau in Brooklyn was quite cooperative. Copies of birth records are on microfilm in Waterford. There are records for all twelve of the children your mother bore. But on your certificate, a different father is listed. You know his name."

Kitty nodded. Very quietly, she said, "Arthur Fitzgerald."

There were audible gasps in the room. John Murphy stood up abruptly.

"What the hell is going on here? he demanded.

"Oh, sit down," Kitty insisted. Then addressing Desmond Joyce, she said, "Years ago, John told me about the man who killed his father. Well, when I told my aunt the story, she turned ghastly white. I pushed her to tell me what was wrong. Finally, she showed me my real birth certificate, one I'd never seen before.

"She said Frank Hines insisted that my mother give me away. My aunt knew the circumstances of my conception. My mother became pregnant with me while Frank Hines was away, working in England. It seems that he didn't send money home regularly, and my mother could barely feed her children. She met Arthur Fitzgerald. He offered to pay her rent and buy food if she would clean his house, cook his meals and grant him other favors... That's how I was conceived. I never blamed her. She did what she had to do."

Kitty assumed something akin to her former attitude. With a toss of her head, and shoulders squared, she faced her husband.

"Now you know why I didn't want to make this trip, and I wanted nothing to do with your search for Arthur Fitzgerald."

She snickered, but there were tears in her eyes.

"My father killed yours."

John Murphy had no reply. He and Mary looked at each other, then at Kitty, but said nothing.

Chapter 51

Inspector Joyce addressed John and Kitty.

"Your friends, the Burkes, mentioned the name of Arthur Fitzgerald, yes?"

"They did, and I recognized it immediately," John Murphy answered.

Quietly, Kitty Murphy said, "So did I."

Looking directly at John, the inspector asked, "Did you intend to kill him?"

"No!" Murphy responded vehemently. "And we didn't. You know that. Not Mary, not Kitty, not me. You must know who did kill him."

Mary MacGregor demanded, "Tell us who killed him!"

Emma held her breath. She dreaded hearing him answer this question. She didn't think she could deal with the repercussions that were sure to come. She needn't have worried.

Desmond Joyce shook his head 'no'.

"I can't tell you that," he said. "That has to remain confidential, as does the reason he was killed. As I said, there's much more to this case than you realize."

Then the inspector focused his attention on Jean Blair.

"Miss Blair," he said, "Tell me about your father."

Jean flustered and protested, "But he's been dead so many years! What could matter now?"

"He came to Stranraer from Onish, near the highlands, I believe," Joyce proposed.

"He did, sir. He came to Stranraer in 1929," Jean said.

Desmond Joyce continued, saying, "He ran away from the Highland Police, I believe."

Jean was stunned.

"No, no, not my father," she protested. Her eyes welled with tears.

The inspector adopted a softer tone of voice, but continued, "It seems that your father was a daring young man. He was accused of robbing a jewelry store in Onish. He ran away before he could be brought to trial."

Here, the inspector smiled benevolently.

"Anyway, he seems to have straightened up once he got to Stranraer. Your father was Ian Blair, correct?"

Jean Blair nodded her head quietly, too astounded to say a word.

"And you," he said, facing Gwillam Morgan. "Since your juvenile skirmish with the law, you haven't had so much as a traffic ticket."

Morgan seemed annoyed at the mere mention of his juvenile arrest, but he said nothing. He checked his watch instead, and Desmond Joyce took the hint.

Turning to Emma, he said, "Mrs. Quinn, as far as I'm concerned, these people are free to leave. Is there anything you require of them?"

"They need to settle their accounts. Nothing more," she responded.

The inspector smiled at her.

"Excellent" he said.

Then, addressing the guests, he directed, "Plan to leave immediately after breakfast tomorrow. And Mrs. Houlihan—Frances, if I may—perhaps you could stay here with Emma one more night?"

"I already planned ta do jest that!"

Chapter 52

On Saturday morning, June ninth, Tommy Quinn's body was prepared for viewing. Emma Quinn walked over to the undertaker's very early that morning with Tommy's one suit, a clean white shirt and a necktie. It took her no time at all to pick out a coffin for him.

She accepted the undertaker's condolences graciously, all the while hoping she looked genuinely sad. She didn't feel she was grieving, just doing her duty.

Next, she walked to St. Michael Church where she met with Father O'Rourke. Together they selected a burial plot for Tommy and a headstone. When the good father asked if she didn't want to buy a double plot, one side for Tommy now, one for her later, she delicately declined. There was no way she wanted to spend eternity side-by-side with him.

Emma was already in love with another man; she had his assurance that he loved her, too. When the time was right, they would marry.

She remembered her courtship with Tommy—how exciting it had been to be young and in love with a handsome rascal. The wedding was beautiful. She was happy; that is, until the reception, where he became so drunk that two men had to carry him home and put him to bed.

I should have known then, she thought.

Now Tommy was dead. If she was brave enough, there was another man waiting to be let into her life. She was being given a second chance.

When she arrived back at home, she found Francie cleaning up the breakfast table.

"Are they gone?" Emma asked.

"Ya mean yer guests?" Francie was looking even more indignant than usual. Arms akimbo, she started chastising Emma.

"While you was out gallavantin', those five upstairs kept me 'oppin'. 'More tea, more jam, more, more, more!' I'm glad they're leavin'. I need a break."

Emma had to chuckle at her. She said, "You're a good friend, Fran. What would I do without you?" She gave her friend a warm hug.

"Yeah, yeah," Francie dismissed the compliment. "Sit down," she said. "I'll get ya a cuppa."

She poured the tea for Emma, and then remembered, "Yer guests 've paid up. Murphy tried ta pay with an American Express card, but I tole 'im, nothin' doin'. Cash only."

"Did he have the cash?" Emma asked, still smiling. She could imagine the argument between Fran and John Murphy. He hadn't stood a chance.

Francie assured her that Murphy had to dig deep into both pants pockets and his wife's purse, but he came up with enough money. And no, the guests hadn't left yet, but they'd be leaving shortly.

"By the way," she preened, "Ya 'ad a phone call."

"Oh?"

"Ya sure did!" Francie was smug.

"Well now, why don't you just tell me about it," Emma teased.

"Mebby I will, mebby I won't."

"Alright. You win." Emma succumbed good-naturedly. "Please, Fran, who called?"

"'oo else! Inspector Joyce!"

Emma could feel her cheeks burning.

"What did he want?" she asked, trying to sound nonchalant.

Her friend smirked, "You!"

"Stop that! Be nice!"

Pleased with herself, Francie grinned. "'e left a bunch a numbers so's ya could ring 'im up if ya was of a mind ta. And 'e says I'm ta stay 'ere one more night, if possible."

"Give me the numbers, if you please," Emma said, "And this will be the last night. You won't need to stay here after tonight."

"Good thing," Francie stated. "er else folks 'll be talkin' about you 'n me instead o' you 'n 'im."

Chapter 53

Emma went to her room. She needed privacy and quiet to think about her situation. She felt no pain thinking about Tommy's death. She hadn't loved him in a very long time. However, despite his actions, despite his reputation, she would honor his memory. She would conduct herself in a respectable way during these next few days. It wasn't in her to dishonor anyone.

Especially, she did not want to do anything to sully Desmond Joyce's reputation. Thinking about him made her realize just how amazing it was, that a man of his caliber, his renown, should love her.

She wanted to phone him. She was afraid to do so. She looked at the list of phone numbers Francie had given her. What if he wasn't at the first number she called? What if someone answering at that number asked her to leave a message? Would she dare to leave her name?

And what if the same thing happened at the second number? And the third? The news would be all over Howth, that she was chasing Inspector Joyce. She didn't dare. There was nothing she needed from him at this moment. She needed to rest.

She lay across her bed and remembered times, early in her marriage, when she and Tommy were young and passionately in love. They had made love on this bed, years ago. She remembered the exquisite pain of achieving the peak of love making. She remembered his delight in her body, her sexuality. Their first few years together had been full of excitement and desire.

When no pregnancy resulted from their passion, Emma began to feel that she was failing Tommy. Every month when her blood flow began, she wept in disappointment. Tommy never seemed to be upset about it though. Once he had even said, "So what, Em? We don't really need kids."

Nevertheless, Emma's desire for a child was strong. She went to see the local doctor and told him of her inability to conceive. He sent her to a gynecologist, a specialist in Dublin, who instructed Emma to take her temperature every morning before arising. He taught her that when her morning temperature dropped lower than her norm and then went higher than her norm the morning after, that meant she had ovulated. This was her fertile time, her best chance to conceive.

Emma explained all this to Tommy. He thought her morning temperature-taking was ridiculous. He said that either babies would come or they wouldn't. He did cooperate, though. They had sex at her most fertile time every month, yet no conception occurred. Often, at that time of her cycle, Tommy was inebriated and their love making was mechanical. She didn't protest, her desire for a baby was that strong.

After six months, Emma returned to the specialist. His opinion was that Emma probably could conceive—she ovulated regularly; the fault was no doubt Tommy's, and nothing could be done for a sterile man.

Emma told Tommy what this doctor had said. She couldn't guess what his reaction would be, but the response she got was devastating. He said, "I knew it all along."

"You what?" she demanded, stunned and confused.

"I said, I knew it," he repeated, with no sign of apology. "My ma told me. When I was fourteen, I had the mumps. That left me sterile. Anyway, the doctor said it probably would. I guess we've proven him right."

She had never forgotten the pain of that moment. Lying on her bed, fifteen years later, it came back just as raw and searing as the first time. He had essentially lied to her, marrying her under false pretenses. She had gone to Father O'Rourke, asking about an annulment of her marriage, but found it wasn't possible. So she had gone through the motions of marriage, kept house, cooked, took an active part in her church's activities, opened her bed and breakfast establishment. Tommy became an obvious alcoholic and never troubled her for sex.

A part of her spirit had died. That is, until four days ago.

chapter 54

Emma Quinn took one last look at the body of her dead husband. Tommy had died in the late afternoon hours of Friday, June eighth, 1968. Now it was Monday, June eleventh, and Tommy was about to be buried. She turned away from his coffin as someone closed the lid. She walked out of St. Michael Church, arm in arm with Frances Houlihan.

Emma hadn't cried at all during the past three days. She didn't feel sad, she didn't feel bereaved. She was simply doing what had to be done.

She certainly didn't feel numb. In fact, her body and soul felt more alive today than she could ever remember, for last night she had lain with her lover.

Desmond rang her up last evening, just to make sure she was alright, he said. But when she heard his voice, she forgot her concern about his reputation. He professed his love for her and how much he wanted her to be his wife. Without hesitation, she asked him to come to her. Minutes later, he arrived at her home. She watched for him from the parlor window, and when he arrived, she took him upstairs to her bed.

They made love as slowly and gently as two people who had loved each other all their lives. She hadn't known that a man could be so tender, so desirous of giving her pleasure. His huge hands stroked her body, and when she moaned with delight, his hand returned to the area that had stirred her.

Through the whole experience, she loved his touch, the taste of his skin and the feel of him on top of her and inside her.

They slept in each other's arms until early morning, when he left.

Thank God for him, she thought, without a modicum of guilt.

On Friday, when Desmond had told her of Tommy's crime, she'd had a hard time believing that her husband was capable of such a thing. Not that she thought she was being lied to—it was just that, as disagreeable as Tommy had always been, never for one minute had she felt afraid of him.

She was shocked to learn that he had been fired from the brewery weeks ago. Tommy always seemed to have money on him. Now she knew where it came from.

The Garda Siochanna was investigating Tommy, but Desmond Joyce had excused himself from the case. First, though, he had cleared all of her guests of suspicion. And imagine, Mary MacGregor and John Murphy were brother and sister. They had come to Ireland to confront Major Arthur Fitzgerald about their father's murder, but they had no involvement in his death.

And Kitty Murphy was the illegitimate daughter of the major. She, too, was innocent of his death.

No, Tommy killed the major. Interpol intended to find out who had paid him to do it and why.

And Desmond…after a respectable time, they would marry. Unless she was pregnant after last night's love making. Then they would marry immediately.

And wouldn't that give Francie something to talk about.

COMING SOON!

Joanne's next novel

The Hallowed Heath

*filled with intrigue, romance and humor;
all set in the beautiful English countryside of the 1950s.*

Here's what the author has to say about her next novel:

"Maiden's Heath is a small town in Surrey, England. To reach it from London, you must drive west on an A road (which is a well-maintained, paved lane), then turn onto a B road (not so well-maintained and often not even paved), and finally pass through a dense woods. North of the woods is a great heath. A coven of witches has lived on the heath for scores of years. Many young women came to the heath to learn the craft, hence the name, *Maiden's Heath*. About a year ago, the Christian brothers from the nearby monastery of St. Edmond drove the women away. They burned the heath, then sanctified it with holy water. However, rumor has it that the witches have returned to the area and intend to reclaim both their heritage and land."

about the author

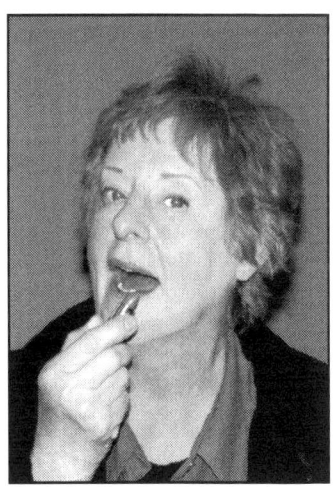

Photo by Carolyn C. Holland

Joanne McGough was born in Pittsburgh, Pennsylvania and now lives in a beautiful, rural Pennsylvania town with her collie and cat. She is a retired registered nurse who specialized in hospice nursing. Joanne loves to sing and is active in the music ministry at her local church. She loves flowers, traveling, cooking, her children, grandchildren and values her friends dearly.

Made in the USA
Charleston, SC
27 June 2012